Also by Will Allison

What You Have Left: A Novel

LONG DRIVE HOME

A Novel

Will Allison

Free Press

New York   London   Toronto   Sydney

Free Press
A Division of Simon & Schuster, Inc.
1230 Avenue of the Americas
New York, NY 10020

First Free Press hardcover edition May 2011

FREE PRESS and colophon are trademarks of Simon & Schuster, Inc.

For information about special discounts for bulk purchases, please contact Simon & Schuster Special Sales at 1-866-506-1949 or business@simonandschuster.com.

The Simon & Schuster Speakers Bureau can bring authors to your live event. For more information or to book an event contact the Simon & Schuster Speakers Bureau at 1-866-248-3049 or visit our website at www.simonspeakers.com.

Designed by Carla Jayne Jones

Manufactured in the United States of America

5   7   9   10   8   6   4

Library of Congress Cataloging-in-Publication Data

ISBN 978-1-4165-4303-9
ISBN 978-1-4516-0819-9 (ebook)

For Deborah and Hazel

LONG DRIVE HOME

Dear Sara,

It's hard for me to imagine the person you'll be when you read this—probably on your way to college and a life of your own. Sometimes that feels like forever away. But other times—when you get into the car wearing your mom's perfume, or shush me distractedly as you study the menu at a diner, or manage to throw a baseball that goes exactly where you want it to—I feel time racing by so fast I can hardly breathe. Not knowing where things will stand between us ten years from now or how this letter will change them, I need to make sure you understand, before I go any further, how grateful I am to have you in my life, how lucky I am to be your father, how sorry I am for the way things have turned out between your mom and me since the accident. I know it's been hard. I know it's been confusing. My intention here is to be honest with you about all of it, to write down for later all the things I can't very well tell an eight-year-old now.

You may be wondering why I'm doing this. I won't pretend I'm not hoping you'll forgive me, but please don't think I'm asking for forgiveness, or that I think I deserve it. Detective Rizzo once told me that all confessions boil down to one thing: stress. People confess, he said, to relieve the psychological and physiological effects of guilt, regret, anxiety, shame. To share the burden with someone else. To at least glimpse the possibility of redemption. It's only human nature.

Remember the time you spilled orange juice on my keyboard and I didn't know why it wasn't working and you told me what you'd done, even though you could have gotten away with it? You said you couldn't stop thinking about it. You said you felt so bad, you had *to tell me, even if you got in trouble. That's where I am. People confess when their need for relief overrides their instinct for self-preservation. I don't claim to be any different.*

Still, I'm not sure I'd be writing this if I didn't also believe that, on some level, you already know the truth about the accident. You were there, after all. I have to think someday it's all going to come clear to you, and when it does, you'll know not only why I did what I did, but also that I wasn't honest with you about it. You don't deserve to be lied to. I don't want that between us, not on top of everything else. I don't want to make the same mistakes with you that I made with your mom.

———

Things didn't have to turn out the way they did. The accident was no more a matter of destiny than anything else you can rightfully call an accident, just mistakes and poor judgment. With a different choice here or there—and I'm talking the small ones you wouldn't otherwise give a second thought to—I could have gotten us safely home from school like I did every other day. Sara would have done her homework at the kitchen table while I prepped dinner, then we might have gone for a bike ride over to Ivy Hill

Park, or played catch in the backyard, or worked on a jigsaw puzzle. She'd have kept me company in the basement while I folded laundry, or read a book on the rug in my office while I returned calls and checked email. At 6:38 sharp, we'd have gotten back into the station wagon to go meet Liz's train, then the three of us would have sat down to stir fry or spaghetti and meatballs and talked about the positions Liz was trying to fill at the bank, or whose parents we wanted to spend Thanksgiving with. Mostly, though, we'd have talked about Sara—which one of her friends she wanted the next play date with, what she wanted to be for Halloween, whether she was going to keep growing her hair or get it chopped off. Putting her to bed, Liz and I might even have paused to remark on how lucky we were, as we were inclined to do, but at no point would we have considered the possibility that we'd dodged a bullet that day, that we'd come *this close* to our lives veering permanently off course. That's the kind of thing you see only in hindsight.

This was late October, just over two years ago, when Sara was in first grade. I had a small accounting business I ran out of the house—tax work, mostly—and I'd knocked off early to be the parent helper in Sara's classroom. Up until the drive home from Montclair, it was a good afternoon. The kids were writing their own historically accurate

Thanksgiving play, with deer meat instead of turkey and no black clothes or funny buckles. I got to help with the script ("Do not be confused, sir, we are Pilgrims, not Puritans!") and painting the backdrop. At the end of the day, there was a birthday party outside. The weather was warm for fall—kids shedding hoodies, kicking up leaves, the sun almost white against a deep blue sky—and though it was Thursday, I remember it feeling like Friday. The birthday girl had brought a box of chocolate cupcakes the size of softballs. Sara offered me a bite of hers, very polite in front of her teacher, and looked relieved when I said no thanks.

I was teasing her about that on the drive home, asking if she'd saved me any, when I had to stop short for a light on Thomas Boulevard. I didn't know there was a police car behind us until it almost rear-ended us. In the mirror, I could see the officer back there cursing me. I shook my head. What are you going to do, I thought, write me a ticket for *not* running the light?

What he ended up doing was backing up and going around us, as if the law didn't apply to him—no flashing lights, no siren, no nothing. He ran the light because he could, because who was going to stop him? As he passed us, he shot me a look. The look was what did it. Imagine my finger tapping the first in a line of dominos. I opened the window, stuck out my arm, and flipped him off.

*   *   *

4

I admit, I'm not the most laid-back driver, especially with Sara in the backseat. Even now, I still think about a close call we had in Cleveland not long before she was born. I'd just passed my CPA exam, and Liz had taken me out to celebrate. On the way home after dinner, a few blocks from our apartment, the light turned green and she started into the intersection. Next thing I knew, the trees and cars and buildings were going sideways. A delivery truck had run the light and spun us into a pole. It felt like we'd been hit by a tornado. The front end of the car was practically gone. A few more feet into the intersection, and it would have been the driver's-side door. Liz was hysterical—"Oh my God! Oh my God!"—hyperventilating and holding her stomach, saying she should have seen the guy coming. She was seven months pregnant.

At the risk of offering too tidy an explanation, it was the kind of thing that makes you appreciate waking up every morning, but also the kind of thing that can make you edgy just driving to the store for a gallon of milk, or watching a lead-foot cop run a light.

Three years later, after we'd paid twice as much for a house in South Orange that was half as big as the one we'd left in Cleveland, the driver of the moving truck, taking a smoke break behind the semi trailer, warned me about Jersey drivers. The lowest of the low, he called them. He was from the city, he said, and therefore in a position to know.

I remember thinking, oh please. I'd heard the jokes about New Jersey and frankly didn't believe motorists in one place were any worse than in another. The next few weeks changed my mind, though. I'd never seen so much hostile, reckless, flat-out incompetent driving. Running the gauntlet to and from Sara's school—twenty-five minutes each way, twice a day, part of the price we paid to send her to a crunchy private school—I'd pass the time tallying infractions and coming up with theories to explain it all. Maybe New Jersey, with its sky-high taxes and neglected roads, simply had more pissed-off drivers than other states. Or maybe New Jerseyans, with their second-highest-per-capita income, felt traffic rules were beneath them. Maybe, living in the shadow of New York City, they suffered a collective inferiority complex that found its outlet on the road. Maybe the police were to blame, for letting them get away with anything they pleased. Or maybe it was our politicians, for being so corrupt that nobody respected the law anymore.

Obviously, I got carried away. Maybe even a little obsessed. Too much time in the car can do that.

The officer didn't notice me flipping him off, or if he did, he didn't care.

"What are you doing?" Sara said.

"Nothing," I told her. "Waving to the policeman."

The patrol car was already a block away.

"The light's green," she said.

A black Suburban in the oncoming lane was turning left in front of us, a tricked-out model with four wheels in back instead of two. Halfway through its turn it stopped, blocking our path. I thought the driver must be lost, or having second thoughts about turning, or car trouble. I couldn't see anything through the tinted windows. It wasn't until he came around the tailgate with his middle finger up, glaring out from under a Yankees cap, that everything clicked into place.

"Yo," he said. "You giving me the finger?"

He was a big guy, maybe thirty, with a green Puma track suit and bloodshot eyes. Stoned, probably. He also happened to be black, which wouldn't matter except that Juwan was too, and I've always wondered, as much as it shames me, if that was a factor in what happened later.

I held up my palms to show him I'd meant no harm. "The cop," I said, "not you."

He glanced over his shoulder, unimpressed; the cruiser was long gone.

Common sense kicked in. I locked the doors. But before I could get the window up, he was sticking his finger in my face.

"Apologize, bitch."

I stared straight ahead and took a deep breath, arms spring-loaded, ready to put the car in reverse. My teeth were clenched so hard they hurt.

"Dad?" Sara said.

"It's okay, honey. Just a misunderstanding."

The guy lowered his finger—yes, I thought, thank you, there's a *child* in the car—but then he unzipped his jacket. I didn't have to turn to see the pistol in his waistband. The dark grip stood out against the white of his T-shirt. The gun rose and fell with his breathing. By now traffic was weaving around us. Someone started honking.

"Don't make me repeat myself," he said.

I told him I was sorry.

"Can't hear you."

"I'm *sorry*."

He laughed. "You got that right."

As I watched him drive off, my legs were shaking so much I could barely keep my foot on the brake. What kind of psychopath flashes a gun with a kid around? I wished I'd closed the window on his arm and dragged him, pushed him into traffic with my door, grabbed for the gun and fired it down his pants. Instead, I'd sat there apologizing.

I turned down the side street and went after him, fumbling for my phone. I had an idea that I'd follow him until the police caught up. If he saw us before then and stopped, I'd run him down. I'd tell the police it was self-defense.

"Dad," Sara said. "What's happening? Where are we going?"

And just like that, I snapped out of it. I pulled over as the Suburban rounded a corner up ahead and told Sara not to worry, everything was fine. I couldn't stand seeing her afraid.

"Can we go home now?"

"Soon, honey. I just have to make a call."

It wasn't until I was standing on the sidewalk dialing 911 that it hit me: I hadn't gotten the license plate. By then I had no hope of catching up with him. I could have filed a report anyway, but I knew no cop was going to drive around looking for a random black Suburban. And what if they sent the officer I'd just seen?

So that's the frame of mind I was in the first time Juwan Richards almost killed us. Sara must have known I was upset, because she didn't say a word until we were almost home. She was eating grapes left over from lunch. I could feel her watching me.

"Still awake back there?" I said, cheerfully as I could.

"Dad? Why'd that man show you his finger?"

I told her it was just a way of telling somebody you're angry.

"But why was he so angry?"

"He was angry at *me*," I said, "because he thought I was angry at *him*. Isn't that strange?"

"He went like *this*!" she said, raising her finger and screwing up her face.

At least Liz wasn't there. Telling her what happened was going to be bad enough. She'd want the guy locked up, immediately, and if it took the whole sheriff's department to bring him in, so be it.

I was putting my window down for some fresh air, thinking maybe I wouldn't mention the gun, when I noticed the convertible in the opposite lane, a Jaguar with its top down. It was accelerating so fast I could hear it coming. Behind the convertible was a police safety checkpoint. Officers were standing in the middle of South Orange Avenue, directing some cars into a lane marked off by neon cones, letting others pass. A couple of cones had been knocked over, and it occurred to me that the convertible might be trying to dodge the police. I started to make the turn into our neighborhood, half looking for signs of a chase, when the convertible turned onto Kingsley too, veering across three lanes of traffic and cutting us off. There was nowhere for me to go. I stood on the brake so hard I came up out of my seat. My sunglasses hit the windshield. Sara cried out as her seat belt locked across her chest. The kid driving the Jaguar—that was my first glimpse of Juwan—didn't so much as turn his head. He was steering with one hand and holding his phone walkie-talkie style with the other. I don't think he ever saw us.

Even as I watched the convertible make another quick turn at the end of the block, I couldn't believe we'd missed each other. It was that close. My heartbeat was pounding in my ears. The stop had thrown me back against the seat, but I still felt like I was pitching forward. I managed to turn around and ask Sara if she was all right. She nodded through a curtain of wavy blond hair, but she was crying and rubbing her shoulder.

"My grapes," she said.

They were all over her lap, the floor, even the dash.

The second time Juwan almost killed us came less than a minute later. At that point, I was feeling like I'd been shot out of a cannon and wasn't coming down anytime soon. "Is this the craziest drive ever, or what?" I was saying, trying to downplay it for Sara, take her mind off her shoulder. I wanted to get us home. In the time it took to reach our street, though, Juwan had made a loop through the neighborhood, and suddenly there he was again, headed toward us. I don't think I'd ever seen anyone driving so fast on our street. We lived in a sleepy little enclave of shady lanes and tidy 1920s-era homes, a neighborhood so quiet that the local driving schools routinely used it for lessons, the kind of place where you felt okay letting your first-grader ride her bike around the block alone. And here was this joker, practically flying. You son of a bitch, I thought. And then, instead of laying on the horn or just letting him pass, I lashed out. It was instinct, more a reaction than a decision. I cut the wheel to the left—as if I were going to turn in front of him into our driveway—then back to the right, to get out of the way.

I was trying to give him a scare, slow him down, teach him a lesson. I figured at worst he'd slam on the brakes. Instead, he swerved into *our* lane, like he meant to squeeze past us on the other side. But since we were still there, not actually turning, he kept swerving—until his front tire caught the curb. The rest happened in a blink. His back end came around, the car went up on two wheels, and just like that it was rolling side over side, coming right at us.

———

Later, you told me it happened too fast for you to be scared. I had enough time to be scared but not enough to appreciate what a mistake I'd made. That didn't sink in until afterwards. Even now, more than two years later, I can hardly admit it to myself, the danger I put you in. Sometimes I look at you and it comes back to me like a sharp blow to the chest.

———

I was twisted around in my seat. Sara was looking at me and saying something, but the sound of the car hitting the tree was still in my ears. Turns out that's what had saved us, one of the big sycamores along the curb. Sara had to say it again: "Dad, you're squeezing me." I *was* squeezing her. I had her by the wrist. When it had seemed the car would end up on top of us, I'd reached for her in the backseat, as if there were a thing in the world I could have done.

Now I let go, thinking *thank God* but also *oh my God*. Sara wiped her eyes and looked at the convertible lying upside down in our neighbor Clarice's yard. The soft top had come loose, its fabric and metal frame sticking out from under the car like a broken wing. There were silvery hollows where the headlights had been.

"He knocked down the gaslight," she said.

I watched the sagging windshield for any sign of the driver. Only when I spotted an orange sneaker next to the car did it hit me, the fact that I actually might have killed someone. And even as the thought flashed through my head, I couldn't believe it. The idea that my actions could have caused the death of another human being was even more preposterous than the idea of somebody walking away from that wreck alive. I told Sara to stay in the car.

"No," she said, tugging at her seat belt. "Wait."

Before I could decide what to do, Clarice was next to our car, frantic in her blue bathrobe, saying something about a boy lying in her yard. I didn't see a boy, but I saw the phone in her hand and understood the police would be there soon. My first impulse was to drive away. The car was still running, still in gear; if only she hadn't been there, all I would have needed to do was lift my foot off the brake.

"Clarice," I said, getting Sara out of the car. "Can you watch Sara?"

I hardly knew Clarice—she was some kind of professor at Seton Hall, or retired professor, and seemed never to get dressed—but she gave a quick nod and put an arm around

Sara. I told Sara not to worry, I'd be right back. By then our mail carrier and a guy in gray sweats with a little dog were coming across the street. They were both on their phones too. They stopped short of the convertible, and when I came around the tree, I saw why. There was a body on the lawn between them—facedown, elbows out, legs crossed at the ankles. It took me a moment to realize it was the driver, that he'd been thrown from the car and not hit by it. He wore a plaid flannel shirt over a brown hooded sweatshirt, loose jeans, argyle socks. One orange sneaker was missing. The dog walker was telling the mail carrier not to touch him, his neck might be broken.

"Is he dead?" I said.

"Don't know," the mail carrier said.

The guy in sweats shifted his dog, a Yorkie, from one arm to the other, juggling his phone. "They want to know if he's breathing."

The mail carrier got down on all fours. Juwan's head was cocked at a funny angle, and the shape of it was all wrong, with a dent on one side and a bulge on the other. A thin line of blood was coming out of his ear.

"Can't tell," the mail carrier said. "Maybe we should turn him over."

"Are you crazy?" the dog walker said.

Juwan's blood was dripping into the grass. I stepped back onto Clarice's driveway, dizzy and breathless. The Halloween skeleton on her front door clattered in the breeze. Across the street in our yard, Sara was holding Clarice's hand and eating a candy bar, looking shell-shocked. I figured she must have picked it up off the ground, which I now saw was littered with debris from the Jaguar—sunglasses, empty water bottles, spiral notebooks, CDs sparkling in the sun. I shouted for her to drop it. She stopped chewing and stared at me.

"What I want to know," the dog walker said, "is what a kid like that is doing with a Jag."

"Wait," the mail carrier said. "I think I got a pulse."

Seeing his fingers on Juwan's wrist, I made the mistake of letting myself believe he might make it. The dog walker relayed the news into his phone, then corrected the dispatcher: "No, no. I said *maybe* a pulse." His dog started to bark. Across the street, Sara was holding the candy bar halfway to her mouth, still trying to figure out what my problem was.

A police car got there first, then an ambulance from the village rescue squad. Hearing the sirens made me want to run, but I stayed where I was until an officer told us to make way for the EMTs. One of them was carrying a duffel bag and a long yellow board with straps and buckles dangling from it. The other one, who didn't look much older than Juwan, asked if anyone had moved the body.

"No way," the dog walker said.

We stood back as she clapped her hands over the body. "Hello in there," she said. "Anybody home?"

Two more squad cars were coming down the street, lights and sirens going. Sara had her hands over her ears. The older EMT fitted Juwan with a neck brace while the woman held a stethoscope to his back.

"Nothing," she said. "Let's roll him."

She put a hand on either side of his head and counted to three; her partner took him by the thigh and shoulder. As they turned him onto the board, I caught a glimpse of his face. I wished I hadn't. There were raccoon bruises around his eyes; clear liquid was leaking from his nose. The older EMT, immobilizing Juwan's head with foam pads, said something about a skull fracture. The woman got a tube in Juwan's mouth, attached a bag, and started squeezing. Juwan's chest rose and fell, as if he were only sleeping.

She'd just switched over to pushing on his chest when another ambulance arrived, this one with two paramedics from the hospital. They called off the EMTs, cut Juwan's shirt open, and hooked him up to a monitor with wires they attached to his chest.

"Okay, sir," a tall officer said to me. "I need you over there."

The dog walker and mail carrier had already joined a group of neighbors in front of our house. I started down Clarice's driveway but looked back as I reached the street. One of the paramedics was peeling off his rubber gloves. The other was saying something into a radio on his shoulder. He checked his watch, disconnected the bag from Juwan's mouth, and pulled the wires off his chest. By the time

I understood what was happening, they were already covering him with a sheet.

"Wait a minute," I said. "He just had a pulse."

The paramedics weren't happy about the way things had turned out, either. The one with the radio gave me a hard look as he closed a kit full of folding plastic shelves. "There's nothing we can do," he said. "He was already dead."

I looked around to see if I was the only one who hadn't lost his mind. The EMTs were no help. Neither was the mail carrier. A hand came to rest on my shoulder. It was the policeman again.

"All right now," he said.

His voice was gentle, as if he were trying to talk me down from a rooftop. I could feel the other cops watching me too, and I wanted to cooperate, but my feet wouldn't move, so I just stood there staring at Juwan. Under the sheet, he somehow seemed smaller. It could have been anybody under there. It could have been Sara.

The officer escorted me halfway across the street, then turned me loose and stood there to make sure I kept going. Sara wasn't in front of the house anymore. I knew she was with Clarice, but I didn't like not knowing where. A fire truck had arrived, and the firefighters were checking out the Jaguar and the downed gaslight. The police had barricaded each end of the block with flares and a cruiser. On the sidewalk in front of our house, a sergeant was asking for eyewitnesses. The gun on his belt made the Suburban guy's look like a toy.

"Here's your man," the dog walker said.

The sergeant looked up at me from a metal box that doubled as a clipboard. "You saw it?"

My mind went blank. I was afraid to speak. I remember telling myself people didn't go to prison for accidents. Then again, just because I hadn't meant to hurt anyone didn't mean what I'd done was accidental.

"That's my car," I said. "He almost hit us."

The sergeant didn't need details. He took down some information from my driver's license and told me to stick around until the detectives got there.

"Can I wait inside?" I said. "I live here."

"Fine by me."

Another officer was calling to him from across the street. As he turned to go, a few of the neighbors asked me what happened. I wanted to tell them it was all the kid's fault—he'd gone and gotten himself killed—but I was sure they'd see through me as soon as I opened my mouth.

"Drinking, probably," the mail carrier said. He nodded toward the officer who'd called out to the sergeant; he was holding what looked like a pint bottle.

Clarice had taken Sara around back to the swing set. When I found them there, she ran to me, asking if the boy had died.

"I didn't know what to tell her," Clarice said.

I explained that he was already dead when the doctors got there.

"Was it our fault?" she said. "Did we make him crash?"

The question almost stopped my heart. "Of course not."

Clarice gave me a sympathetic look and asked if Sara could have another candy bar. The pocket of her bathrobe was bulging with them.

"Can I?" Sara said.

I was so relieved by that look of Clarice's, I would have let Sara eat them all. "Sure," I said, wanting to get her into the house before she talked to anyone else. "But then we need to call Mom."

We didn't make it, though. The sergeant was coming up the driveway with three other men. "Here you are," he said. "We've been ringing the bell out front." He introduced a traffic investigator and two detectives, Johnson from the village police department and Rizzo from the county prosecutor's office. Glancing at their badges, I had no hope of their believing anything I might say. This is it, I thought. It's over.

Rizzo said they'd need me to stop by the station to give a full statement later on, once they were done working the scene. "For now, could you just show us what happened?"

I steadied my hands on Sara's shoulders and stared at the crooked part I'd combed into her hair that morning, willing her to keep quiet. "Sure. I was about to take my daughter inside."

"I want to stay," Sara said.

19

Rizzo squatted down to her level. He had close-cropped, wiry hair that almost matched his charcoal suit. "What's your name, young lady?"

She mumbled around the candy bar.

"I'm glad to meet you, Sara," he said. "Would it be all right if we borrow your dad for five minutes?" He took off his wristwatch and handed it to her.

Sara held the thick, gold band, stared at the dial. She didn't know how to tell time, but I knew she wouldn't tell Rizzo that. "Okay."

I let her into the house, then followed Rizzo back down the driveway, where the traffic investigator was asking Clarice if she was the property owner. She cinched her bathrobe.

"If you mean is that my house, yes, it is," she said.

The police had cleared the street, moving everyone behind the barricades. Two TV news trucks were parked there too.

"Whenever you're ready," Rizzo said.

I tried to imagine how the accident might have looked from where we were standing, whether it would have been clear what I'd done. Not that telling the truth crossed my mind, though—not so long as Sara and I were the only ones who'd seen what happened.

I kept my explanation short. I didn't mention the first time we'd seen Juwan, over on Kingsley, because I didn't want them thinking I might have had it in for him. I just said we'd been on the way home from school and indicated which direction I'd been coming from, where I'd turned, where I stopped when I saw the convertible. I explained how the car had hit the curb and started to roll.

"It was like a football," I said. "You couldn't tell which way it was going to bounce."

"Any idea why he lost control?" Rizzo said.

I shook my head. My throat was so dry I was having trouble talking. Someone had apparently pointed me out to one of the reporters. From behind the barricade, she tried calling me over. A guy with a big camera on his shoulder was standing next to her. Sara was at the window, holding Rizzo's watch. I held up a finger to let her know we were almost done, then asked the detectives when I should come to the station. Rizzo said from the look of things it would be two or three hours, minimum.

"Meanwhile," he said, nodding toward the news trucks, "I'd steer clear of them."

I needed to find out how much Sara knew. We gave Rizzo his watch back, then went up to her room and opened the window so we could hear what was going on.

"See how the detectives are taking pictures?" I said, sitting next to her on the bed. "They're trying to figure out why he crashed."

"I feel bad for the boy," she said, "but I also feel bad for the tree. Trees are living things, too."

21

From up there, the damage to the tree didn't look so bad. A few scrapes and gouges. "Don't worry," I said. "It'll be fine."

"Not the boy, though."

"No," I said, wishing they'd hurry up and take him away. Then I asked Sara why she'd thought the crash was our fault.

"I didn't. I just wasn't sure."

"He was probably drunk. That's why a lot of crashes happen."

She nodded. She knew about being drunk from an episode of *Little House on the Prairie* we had on DVD—the terrible things it could make a person do. She was rubbing her shoulder. I pushed up her sleeve to see if the seat belt had left a bruise.

"Do you think I did anything wrong?" I said.

"Like what?"

Our cat, Chairman Meow, had jumped onto the windowsill. I reached over to scratch his chin. I didn't want to put ideas into her head.

"I bet he was drunk *and* on the phone," she said. "Mom says talking on the phone when you're driving is against the law."

"We should call her." I went ahead and dialed Liz. I told her there had been an accident on our street, that the driver was dead, that I had to give a statement at the police station and probably wouldn't be able to meet her train.

"Wait a minute," she said. "Sara saw somebody *die*?"

I had to talk her out of coming straight home.

"Can I at least speak to her?" she said. I handed Sara the phone. Three times Liz asked how she was doing, and three times Sara said she was fine. Then Liz asked her to put me back on. "Is she really all right?"

The medical examiner's van was at the curb, waiting. When the detectives finished photographing Juwan and using a tape measure to mark his location, they helped the examiner zip him into a bag.

"How is he going to breathe in there?" Sara said.

"He can't breathe, sweetie, remember? He died."

"Oh, yeah."

Then she asked where they were taking him, and I tried to explain what a morgue was. Meanwhile, the traffic investigator was going door to door, looking for witnesses. Rizzo brought out his camera again. Down by the barricade, the dog walker was giving an interview. Sara left the room and came back holding a box of Band-Aids.

"Are you bleeding?" I said.

"They're not for me. They're for the tree."

"I told you, the tree's fine."

I opened the curtains wider. Rizzo had started taking pictures of our car, and it made me nervous to think he considered it part of the accident scene. Sara asked if she could go over. I said no. She asked if I'd take her. I said maybe later. She said she was going now.

"Please, sweetie," I said, "I'm busy here."

Then suddenly she was crying, saying I didn't care about her or the tree. I should have been paying more attention to her.

"Look," I said, pulling her onto my lap. "Those Band-Aids aren't going to do the trick, okay? What we need is some gauze." I promised her we'd bandage the tree later, after the police were gone. I turned back to the street. I'd thought Rizzo was done with our car, but now I saw him in our yard, getting it from another angle.

Not long after they took Juwan away, Detective Johnson, the one from the village police, left in a patrol car with a uniformed officer. It was starting to get dark. The police brought out generator-powered floodlights that lit up the whole street. I turned off the bedroom light. Sara was watching TV, which was keeping her occupied enough that I could stay at the window, waiting to see if they found any witnesses. Our neighborhood was mostly commuters who didn't get home until seven or later, but there were a fair number of stay-at-homers and work-at-homers, not to mention the nannies and kids and yard crews who were usually around in the afternoon. It was hard to believe nobody had seen what happened.

Rizzo and the traffic investigator bagged the last of the debris from Clarice's yard. Things were starting to wind down. A tow truck was waiting at the corner. The sergeant came to the door and asked me to move the station wagon. I pulled into our driveway and watched as they turned the convertible over and winched it to the truck. Then the sergeant had his men take down the barricades. Rizzo said they'd be ready for my statement as soon as Johnson got back from notifying the family. Up until then, I'd managed not to think about Juwan's parents. Now it was starting to sink in, the fact that he wasn't just some anonymous punk. I didn't think I could go through with the statement.

I told Rizzo I was supposed to meet my wife's train and asked if I could come to the station some other time.

He shook his head.

"What about in the morning?"

He said no, they'd be at the morgue. "We have to get somebody from the family down there to ID the body."

I must not have looked so good.

"They don't see the actual body," Rizzo said. "We just show them a Polaroid."

It was barely a mile to the station. I stayed under the speed limit the whole way, in no hurry to get there. The car felt unfamiliar, like when it comes back from the shop and the side mirror is wrong, the seat is too far back, the radio is tuned to someone else's station. An officer named Carla introduced herself to Sara and took her into the break room for ice cream while the sergeant led me to a desk where Rizzo was waiting with Johnson, who looked like he was ready to call it a day. I thought about how it must have been, telling Juwan's parents. I'd heard they bring along a priest—you know why they're there as soon as you open the door. Johnson explained that Rizzo would be taking my statement while he typed it up. He offered me a glass of water, but I said no, not wanting them to see my hands trembling.

Rizzo pressed a button on a cassette recorder, noted the date and time, then asked me to state my name and address.

"Now just start at the beginning," he said.

I could feel my shirt grow damp as I told them more or less what I'd told them earlier, trying not to think about the fact that I was being recorded. I worried about contradicting myself. I worried about seeming worried. They were the police, after all; they dealt with liars every day. I finished up as quickly as I could, saying I didn't know exactly what had happened after the Jaguar started rolling over because I'd turned around in my seat to reach for Sara.

Rizzo referred to his notes. His tone was almost apologetic. "Mr. Bauer, earlier you indicated you didn't know why the driver lost control. Is that correct?"

I nodded, then remembered the recorder. "Yes."

"Could you venture a guess?"

"Maybe he was drunk."

"How fast would you say you were going at the time of the accident?"

"I was getting ready to turn into my driveway," I said, "but then I saw him coming and stopped."

"A full stop?"

"Yes."

Rizzo studied his notepad again, tapping his pen on the page, and then, in the same apologetic tone, he said, "Is it possible he might have thought you were going to turn left in front of him?"

It felt as though they'd already pieced together what happened, even though I couldn't for the life of me imagine how, without another witness. When I shrugged, it felt like there were cinder blocks on my shoulders. "I don't know what he thought."

My face had gone hot, but Johnson didn't even look up from his typing. Rizzo just nodded and moved along to the next question, as if the whole interview were nothing but a formality.

"Did you have your turn signal on?"

"No. Maybe. I don't remember."

"Did you move your vehicle after the crash?"

"No."

"Could you describe the road and weather conditions?"

"Same as when you got there," I said. "Clear day. The road was dry."

"Any other cars on the street?"

"No."

"Any pedestrians in or near the roadway?"

"Not that I saw."

"All right," he said, reaching for the recorder. "That should do it."

Johnson printed out the transcript and had me sign it. Just like that, it was over.

On the way back to the break room, Rizzo asked how Sara was holding up. I said pretty well, considering.

"Mind if I talk to her?"

There was no way I was going to let that happen, but I was afraid he'd be suspicious if I said no.

"She's had a long day."

"Maybe some other time," he said, "but while it's still fresh."

I was glad to see Liz in the break room with Sara on her lap. She had on a black suit and the running shoes she carried in her bag, rubbing Sara's back as she spoke with Carla. She lifted Sara onto her feet when I came in and put her arms around me.

"Hey," she said. "You all right?"

For the first time since the accident, holding her tight, I didn't feel utterly on my own. "Let's get out of here."

Rizzo introduced himself to Liz and said he was sorry for keeping us so late. Then he asked if Sara would like to be a junior detective. She lit up when he pulled an official-looking silver badge from his pocket.

"By the power vested in me," he said, "I hereby thereby such and such do deputize you a junior detective." He pinned on the badge. "Welcome to the force. We could use your help."

_____

There was another reason I didn't want you talking to Rizzo. They have to warn suspects about self-incrimination, but nobody was going to warn you about incriminating me. You would have done it without even realizing. And then you might have ended up blaming yourself for my getting caught. I didn't want you to have to live with that.

On the other hand, though, let's say after you finish this letter, you feel compelled to tell someone what really happened. That would be different. That's a risk I accept. Maybe you'll feel like you have to. Maybe it'll be the only way to clear your conscience.

_____

I was so glad to be out of the police station, I forgot about Juwan and his family just long enough for it to hit me all over again, walking to the car.

"Want me to drive?" Liz said.

"If you don't mind."

She took my hand and then Sara's, and we crossed the parking lot like that, the three of us holding hands.

It was late to be making dinner, so I suggested we stop for pizza before heading home. On the way to the restaurant, I started telling Liz about the accident, but Sara said, "Let me tell it." I sat back and held my breath as she launched into her own pell-mell account. I wanted to hear what she had to say. Better that she let something slip in front of Liz than in front of the police. I didn't have to worry, though. She skipped over our first brush with Juwan, and most of what she said was repeated, stuff she'd overheard. It occurred to me that the accident might have unfolded so fast she hadn't really had a chance to form her own impression. For all I knew, she'd been looking off in another direction and hadn't even seen what happened.

I waited until we got to the restaurant to tell my version, basically the same story I'd told the police. Somehow, with Liz, it felt like even more of a lie. She shut her eyes and pulled Sara close when I came to the part about the Jag almost landing on us.

"I don't know if I can hear this," she said.

"But we're okay, Mom."

"That's all that matters," I said.

Liz stared at the untouched slice of pizza on her plate. "But what if you weren't?"

With the gaslight down, our end of the block was dark, but that didn't stop Sara from taking Liz over to see the tree as soon as we got home. The skeleton on Clarice's door was gone. I rang the bell, explained the situation, and asked if we could bandage the tree. Clarice said of course and turned the porch light on. I went back to our house for a flashlight and the gauze Liz used when she and Sara played doll hospital. When I came out again, Sara was touching the raw places on the tree where the car had broken the bark. She aimed the flashlight and followed me around the trunk as I unspooled the gauze, trying to cover as much of the damage as possible. It got harder near the ground, where the trunk bulged with thick knots. Liz said they reminded her of skinned knees.

Sara said she thought the tree was dying. "All the bark's peeling off, even where the car didn't hit."

"Come on," Liz said, tucking the last of the gauze in on itself. "You've seen sycamores. That's just how they are."

"I'm calling this one Sicky," Sara said. "Sicky Sycamore."

That night, for the first time in her life, Sara asked for a night-light. She said she didn't want to go to sleep because she was afraid she might stop breathing.

"You won't," I said. "I promise."

"But everybody does sometime."

"Only when they're old or hurt. You're young, and I'm not going to let anything hurt you."

After she was in bed, Liz and I watched the local news to see if there was a story about the accident. I was hoping there wouldn't be, but no such luck. A traffic fatality in Newark, just a few blocks away, might not have gotten much notice, but this was quiet, suburban South Orange. They showed footage of the police, the bystanders, the upside-down convertible. You could see our house in the background.

Liz moved closer to me on the sofa. "Why'd it have to happen on *our* street?"

31

The reporter—the same one who'd called out to me—said they hadn't determined the cause of the crash but that alcohol was reportedly involved. That was a relief to hear, but as soon as she started talking about the victim—a high school student, his name wasn't being released—I felt sick. I reached for the remote and turned off the TV.

"And why do people drive like such fucking fools?" I said.

"Was he all bloody?"

"Not really. His head was messed up. The car might have rolled over on him."

"Don't think about it. I shouldn't have asked."

We went upstairs to look in on Sara, who didn't stir as we each kissed her good night again, and then Liz said she was going to bed; she had an early meeting. She'd been having a lot of early meetings since she became HR director that spring. Her bank was trying to buy another bank, just like it had bought her old bank in Cleveland. I remembered how excited we'd been when they'd promoted her to New York. A life on the East Coast had seemed bigger, more promising and exciting. Now I wished we'd never left.

I had a glass of wine before bed, but I still couldn't sleep. I kept going over my conversations with the police, kept worrying what else Sara might say to Liz when the two of them were alone, kept imagining how it must have been for Juwan—the surprise of seeing me come into his lane, the jolt of fear he must have felt as his car struck the curb. I hoped the mail carrier had been wrong about a pulse, that Juwan was dead before he ever could have known what happened.

Around 1 a.m., Sara cried out. Liz and I hurried across the hall and found her sitting up in bed, holding her pillow and crying. She'd had a dream about the tree.

"It got so weak it just fell over," she said. "It landed right on top of the house."

After we got her calmed down, she asked if I'd stay until she fell asleep. Liz went back to bed. Sara rolled over and pulled my arm around her like a blanket. I must have lain there an hour, listening to her breathe and trying not to think of Juwan's empty bed, the night his parents must be having, what it would be like to know your child was never coming home again.

I tucked her in and went downstairs to see if there was anything about the accident online. I tried getting some work done—payroll taxes for a new client, a pharmacy in Short Hills—but I couldn't concentrate. I started a load of laundry. I brushed the Chairman and clipped his claws. I checked online again and looked to see if the paper had come. I went back to the basement to put the laundry in the dryer and empty the dehumidifier. I cleaned the litter box. I made a grocery list, threw out some leftovers, and took out the trash. I sent an email to the mortgage company about an insurance bill that should have been paid out of escrow. I did push-ups and sit-ups on the rug in front of the fireplace.

The paper finally came around five, landing with a faint pop on the sidewalk. It was still dark outside. The sycamore looked like it had been TP'd by someone who didn't know the tissue was supposed to be up in the branches, not around the trunk. I brought the paper in and scanned the local section. Below a story about Seton Hall students getting mugged for their laptops was a brief item about the accident—nothing I didn't already know, but I was glad to see it referred to as a one-car crash. I reread the story and then checked the obituaries, though it was too soon for that. As the words started getting fuzzy, I lay down on the sofa and was just drifting off when I heard Liz's alarm.

By the time I made coffee and got upstairs, Liz was already in the shower. She reached around the curtain for the mug and took a swallow. "You never came back."

I told her I couldn't sleep.

"How about Sara?"

"No more dreams."

"Do you think we should take her to see Kim Lee?"

I sat on the edge of the tub. Kim Lee was a counselor whose kids went to Sara's school. We'd heard she was great, but I didn't want her questioning Sara about the accident.

"I think it's possible to make too big a deal of it."

"But you know how she is," Liz said. "How things can get to her."

I talked Liz into giving it a few days, and when she was done showering and putting her long, dark hair up in a towel, we went in to wake Sara. Every weekday, Liz got up half an hour earlier than she needed to so the two of them would have time to hang out in bed, reading and talking. Normally I'd leave them to themselves—"girl time," Sara called it—but that day I stayed, holding Sara as she told us about her dream again, then opening the curtains so she could see the tree, how strong and sturdy it looked in the morning light.

After Liz left to walk to the train station, I considered calling Sara in sick. I didn't want her out of my sight. I even asked her if she'd like to take the day off, go to a movie or something, but she said her class was rehearsing the play.

I took it easy on the way to school and ended up getting tailgated, honked at, and passed in a no-passing zone by a church van. We hit construction north of the highway, a road closure, but they hadn't marked a detour, and nobody knew where to go. Eventually we came to the intersection where the Suburban guy had stopped us. By then I'd spilled coffee all over my jeans. Sara looked up from one of the kids magazines she kept in the seat-back pocket.

"That man was mean," she said. "I hope we don't ever see him again."

"We won't," I said, remembering the self-satisfied way he'd unzipped his jacket. Who'd have imagined that things could have gotten so much worse, that being threatened with a gun would end up little more than a footnote to the afternoon? At least that's how I thought of it then.

As usual, the streets around Sara's school were chaotic. Cars were double-parked, blocking driveways and hydrants. Parents were trolling for open spots. Kids were everywhere, not just from Sara's school but from the public high school down the street. I walked her upstairs to her classroom. The backdrop I'd worked on the day before was spread out to dry, and I was so sleepy I accidentally stepped on it, leaving a footprint on the forest I'd painted.

Now that we were there, Sara didn't want me to leave. She clung to my arm. I told her she didn't have to talk about yesterday and probably shouldn't.

"But I want to," she said, pulling the detective badge from her pocket. "I brought this for show-and-tell."

I mentioned the accident to her teacher and asked her to call if Sara changed her mind about coming home. Then I hugged Sara, a long hug that embarrassed her, and said good-bye.

On the way downstairs, I ran into Warren, head of the school, wearing an orange vest and carrying a stop sign.

"Got a sec?" he said. The regular crossing guard had just

quit, and Warren was looking for a fill-in until they could hire someone else. "Just a few weeks. It'd count as your parent job for the whole year."

Before the accident, I would have been happy to give up my job shelving books in the school library, but now, I had no interest in being responsible for other people's kids. "Sorry," I said. "I wish I could help, but work's pretty crazy right now."

In fact, work was pretty slow. I killed some time in Montclair, taking the car for an oil change and hoping for a call to come get Sara. Instead, as I was on my way home, Liz called to say she'd made an appointment with Kim Lee.

"I thought we were going to wait," I said.

She said she didn't want to take any chances, and this was the only appointment she could get—a last-minute cancellation we should be grateful for.

At that point, I didn't see any way out of it. "Then good," I said. "The sooner, the better."

I hung up as I was turning onto our block. In the time I'd been gone, things had gotten busy on Clarice's side of the street. There was a PSE&G truck with a utility crew repairing the gaslight, plus two pickups and a trailer with rolls of sod. The yard guys had already taken up the grass damaged by the Jaguar and were going over the soil with rakes and rollers. I was glad to see things getting back to normal so fast—until I noticed the tree. Propped against the trunk were a wreath of flowers, a teddy bear, a skateboard. More flowers were piled around a framed portrait of Juwan that I made a point of not looking at too closely. The gauze had been replaced by a white ribbon.

Sara wasn't thrilled about seeing Kim Lee. Her practice was in Verona, in a suite of medical offices above a shopping plaza.

"Can't I just talk to you and Mom?" Sara said as we climbed the stairs.

"Sometimes it's good to talk to someone else."

Sara relaxed a little when she recognized Kim from school, and after Kim and I compared notes on Sara's teacher—Kim's daughter had been in the same class two years earlier—Kim led Sara into a softly lit room with a leather sofa and big chairs. I asked if I could stay, but she said it would be better if she talked to Sara alone, so I stood in the waiting room, trying to listen through the door. There was a radio playing soft rock, just loud enough that I couldn't make out what they were saying. A sign taped to the radio read, "Please do not touch."

At the end of their session, Kim invited me in. Sara was cross-legged on the sofa with crayons and a pad of paper, drawing what looked like an ambulance.

"Do we have to leave right this second?" she said. "I'm not done."

Kim suggested she finish her picture in the waiting room. After Sara was gone, I mentioned her having thought we might have caused the accident. I was hoping to get a sense of what she'd told Kim.

"Actually," Kim said, "she said she was afraid the police might blame you, even though it wasn't your fault."

"Really? She never told me that."

"I think she's still trying to sort it all out." Kim put on a pair of green reading glasses and opened her appointment book to schedule Sara's next session. "Seeing what she saw, trying to understand what dying is—it's a lot for a six-year-old."

By the time we got home, there were more flowers at the tree, another skateboard, a poster with laminated photographs.

"What about the gauze?" Sara said.

I told her we'd bandage the tree again later, when the memorial was gone. She asked if I'd take her over for a look.

"Just for a minute," I said, not wanting to be there when the next person showed up with flowers.

The workers had finished with the lawn and were now replacing damaged shrubs along Clarice's driveway. They greeted us mostly in Spanish but made clear that it was okay to walk on the sod. Sara circled the tree. She looked at the photos. She picked up the teddy bear and hugged it.

Then she got down on her knees, put her hands together, and began to pray.

I was dumbstruck. I'd never seen her pray before. We didn't go to church; we didn't even say grace. The families of the kids in her class, the ones who were religious at all, were so low-key about it that you could hardly tell the Christians from the Jews from the Muslims.

"Are you praying for the tree, or the boy?"

She was moving her lips, but no sound was coming out. The workers were watching us. With nothing else to occupy myself, I glanced at the photos. That's where I first learned Juwan's name and saw what he really looked like. A happy kid. A goofy kid. Most of the shots were candids, he and his friends with skateboards, mugging for the camera. There was also a yearbook picture, a prom photo, a portrait of him in a band uniform holding a trumpet.

I wondered if his parents had been there yet. That morning, as I was driving Sara to school, they'd probably been on their way to the morgue. I imagined a cold hallway, a smell like a high school biology lab, a Polaroid that looked just like their son but also nothing like him at all.

"Dad?" Sara said. "Don't you want to pray too?"

A crowd was gathering in Clarice's yard when we got home from the train station that night. Cars were parked up and down the block.

"Must be some kind of vigil," I said.

Sara asked what a vigil was, and Liz said it's when people stay up at night to remember someone.

I suggested we go out for dinner again, to avoid the scene. "Maybe this'll be over by the time we get back."

"No! I want to see," Sara said.

"I think that would be okay," Liz said.

I looked at her—*Really?*—and she looked right back— *Yes, really. Since when do we hide things from her?*

Inside, the three of us stood at the window. I felt like a vulture, but also as though I couldn't resist. There must have been fifty people out there, teenagers mostly. They were hugging each other, laying flowers at the tree, writing messages on the skateboards. Now and then you could hear the sounds of one of them crying.

Off to the side, a few adults were gathered around a woman in a black dress dabbing her eyes. You couldn't miss her, even at dusk—she was tall, with a full, reddish Afro. I guessed it was Juwan's mom, and the sight of her made his death more real to me than having actually seen the accident. I remember thinking that if I were her, I'd want to kill myself. I couldn't imagine waking up in the morning knowing Sara was dead and feeling like there was a single worthwhile thing left to do in the world. I went into the kitchen and stood at the fridge, pressing my forehead against the smooth, humming metal, trying to block it all out.

"Can we go over?" Sara called after me.

I was relieved to hear Liz telling her no, it was for people who knew him.

"But Clarice is there."

"It's Clarice's yard," Liz said.

"Can't we at least open the window?"

I threw together some bean and cheese burritos, and we ate at the kitchen table, listening in strained silence to what was going on across the street. First they prayed, then they sang. Sara ate half her burrito and asked to be excused so she could go back to the window. She was still there when I finished eating. The crowd had gotten bigger. They were holding candles and singing "Amazing Grace."

"Let's get you ready for bed," Liz said.

Sara sighed. "How am I supposed to sleep with all that singing?"

I scooped her up and started toward the stairs. "It has to end sometime."

That night around two o'clock, long after the vigil, Juwan's mom came back. I was on my way downstairs to the sofa, not wanting to keep Liz up with my tossing and turning, when I happened to look out front. There's no overnight parking allowed on our street, so it was unusual to see a car at that hour. I figured one of the kids had been too torn up to drive home and had gotten a ride with somebody else. Then I realized there was someone *in* the car, so I thought maybe one of them had gone out after the vigil and gotten drunk and ended up back here again. Maybe Juwan's girlfriend. Maybe they'd had a fight—the reason he'd been driving so fast?—and now she was out there wishing she could take back whatever it was she'd said.

But it was the woman from the vigil who got out of the car. I recognized her silhouette in the gaslight's glow. It had gotten cold, but she didn't have a coat, and at first she just stood on the sidewalk, hugging herself. After a while she went over and put one hand on the tree, then the other. She was standing on the flowers but didn't seem to notice. She looked like she was trying to push the tree over. At some point she began to cry. Her head fell, her shoulders shook, her hands balled into fists against the bark. She was sobbing so hard that I could hear her through the window, gasping and wailing as if she were being mauled, having her heart torn out. Watching her was like standing at the edge of a pit I couldn't see the bottom of.

This will sound awful, but I considered calling the police. For her own good, I told myself—she should have been at home with her family. Even if Juwan's dad wasn't in the picture, surely she had siblings, parents, someone to look after her. I was about to turn on a light, thinking she might get self-conscious about waking the neighborhood and leave, when she stopped crying and looked across the street, toward our house. I thought she'd seen me. I stepped behind the curtain, but then I realized she was watching a raccoon make its way along the curb. The sight of it must have spooked her, because when it disappeared down a sewer grate, she got into her car and drove off.

I lay down on the sofa, my heart hammering. I remember feeling like it would serve me right if something terrible happened to my family too. To get what I'd given. That's what I would have wanted, I think, if I had been in her shoes. Chairman Meow settled onto my chest, and I concentrated on his purring, the ticking of the mantel clock, the hiss of the radiator—anything to get the sound of her crying out of my head.

I must have finally drifted off, because the next thing I knew, I was standing in Sara's doorway. It was still nighttime. Liz was there, shaking me.

"Wake up, honey," she said. "Glen. Wake *up*. You're sleepwalking."

She'd heard me coming up the stairs, heavy footfalls that didn't sound right. Like Frankenstein, she said later.

"I am awake," I said.

"What is it?" Sara asked.

"Just checking on you," I said.

The strange thing is, once I came around, I remembered it all—walking up the stairs, opening the door, seeing her curled under the comforter. But I'd done those things without so much as a thought in my head.

"Are you really awake?" Liz said.

"Yes."

"Are you sure?"

"Yes."

She was looking at me like she couldn't trust a word I said. "Then go back to bed," she said, already closing the door. "I'm staying with Sara."

If there had been a lock, I'm sure she would have used it.

I woke groggy and confused, staring out at a gray morning. I'd never sleepwalked before, and it unnerved me. If I could ramble around the house unconscious, what was to stop me from, say, picking up the phone in my sleep and confessing to Rizzo? A light rain began to fall as I drove to the bakery for Liz's favorite cinnamon buns. Except for a handful of weekend commuters heading to the train station, downtown was mostly deserted at that hour on a Saturday. Back at the house, I brought in the paper and was just starting to check the obituaries when Liz came tiptoeing downstairs. I set the paper aside and walked toward her with my arms out, like a zombie.

"Stop it," she said, swatting my arms and trying not to laugh. "You gave me the creeps. It's like your body was there but you weren't."

I told her about Juwan's mom showing up and said maybe that had something to do with my sleepwalking.

"You should see a doctor," she said. "Seriously. What if you'd scared Sara? Or accidentally hurt her?"

"How could I hurt her?"

"People do all kinds of things when they're sleepwalking."

I didn't want to argue. I suggested we spend the rest of the weekend in Philadelphia at her mom's, give things across the street a chance to die down. She reminded me we had plans; we were supposed to go out to dinner with Sara's friend Lacy and her parents.

"Lacy wants to see the tree," Sara said, coming into the kitchen in her nightshirt. "Everybody in my class does."

Liz reached for the obituaries. "Here it is." She looked at me to make sure it was okay and began to read aloud. Juwan Richards had been born and raised in South Orange, she said. He was a senior at the high school, an honor student who hoped for a career in medicine. He worked summers as a lifeguard at the village pool. His hobbies included music and skateboarding.

"And drinking and driving," I said.

Sara's eyes widened in surprise, but I was so intent on trying not to feel anything for Juwan that I didn't care. Ignoring me, Liz continued. Juwan was survived by his mother, Tawana; his father, who lived in Maryland; and an older sister in California. A graveside service was being held the following afternoon, at Rosedale Cemetery.

Sara put down her cinnamon bun. "Can we go?"

"No," I said.

"But I want to see him again. I want to say good-bye."

"Sweetie, he's dead."

"That's why I want to."

"You didn't even know him."

"But Dad—"

A clap of thunder rattled the window. The rain was suddenly a downpour. Sara got up from the table and went into the dining room.

"The teddy bear! The pictures! Everything's getting soaked."

I joined her at the window. The wreath had already blown over, and flowers lay scattered among big brown sycamore leaves on the freshly laid sod.

"Do something!"

"Let's give it a minute," I said, "see if it lets up."

It didn't, though, and soon I was coming back from the basement with a tarp. Sara stood at the door while I jogged across the street, propped up the wreath, and covered as much of the memorial as I could. When the wind blew the tarp off, I came back for rocks from our flowerbed and used them to weigh down the corners. Liz and Sara were waiting at the door with a towel when I was done. Sara hugged me before I even had a chance to dry off, then Liz sent her back to breakfast. As I was taking off my boots, she said maybe the funeral wasn't such a bad idea.

"We're strangers, Liz. Why would we go to his funeral? Anyway, Sara's too young."

"How do you know?"

"Because I was her age when I went to my grandmother's funeral, and it scared the crap out of me."

"I don't think that ever changes," she said. "No matter how old you are."

*   *   *

An hour later, water was pooling in the basement, coming right through the wall in brownish trickles. Liz was still stuck on the funeral.

"I think you're being overprotective," she said, fashioning a makeshift dam of old rags around some moving boxes we'd never unpacked.

"She doesn't even know what she's asking for." I wanted to say, *Now you're giving* me *the creeps.* First the vigil, now the funeral—it was as if she knew I hadn't told her the whole truth about the accident and was messing with me, trying to torture it out of me.

"Can I help?" Sara said, coming down the stairs.

I found a mop for her to push around and was bringing in the shop vac when the doorbell rang. Sara ran back upstairs.

"It's the detective!"

Liz shot me a look of confusion. I tried to seem unconcerned, but my first thought was that he'd come to arrest me. Why else show up unannounced at ten o'clock on a Saturday morning? I started for the door, panic rising in my throat. Rizzo was cupping his eyes to the glass. He straightened up as I came into the vestibule. He had on the same suit as before, as if he hadn't stopped working since Thursday.

"Detective," I said, opening the door, relieved to see he was alone. "I'd like to report a Peeping Tom."

He thought that was funny, or pretended to at least. Then he apologized for disturbing us. "Just had a few follow-up questions and didn't want to drag you down to the station again."

As I was taking his umbrella, Sara came downstairs wearing her badge. She told him she'd decided to be a policeman when she grew up. "A girl can be a policeman, right? Like Carla."

"You bet," Rizzo said. "Police *officer*."

Then she asked to see his gun.

"Why don't you go play in your room?" Liz said. She sounded like she didn't appreciate Rizzo's being there. She brought him a cup of coffee but didn't offer to leave, taking a seat between us at the dining room table. Rizzo didn't seem to mind. He made small talk, complimenting the house and asking how long we'd been there. He said he lived in the village too, not five minutes away.

"I guess this whole thing has you working overtime," Liz said.

He shrugged. "It's not every day I get a red ball in my own back yard."

I asked if the driver had been drinking. He said they wouldn't know for sure until the autopsy report, which could take three to six months.

"Months?" Liz said.

The labs were slow, he explained, and the medical examiner's office was understaffed and overworked. "It's Newark," he said. "Homicides. What are you going to do?" He blew on his coffee and took a sip. "Meanwhile, I'm just trying to rule out everything else besides alcohol. Not jump to conclusions. I mean, at this point, for all we know, it could have been a bee sting. Seriously. One time we had this poor guy, rear-ends a squad car in the rotary down by the train station. Of all the luck, right? Claimed a bee stung him. We're thinking, yeah, sure, buddy. But damned if the guy didn't have a stinger right between his fingers."

"Amazing." Liz glanced at his notepad on the table, clearly wishing he'd get on with it.

"Let's see," he said, taking out a pen. "Meant to ask you Thursday night, Mr. Bauer—were you acquainted with the victim?"

"No."

"Ever seen him before?"

"Not that I know of."

"Recognize his car?"

"No."

And before I had time to worry he'd found out about our first encounter with Juwan, he was on to the next question. "Was he driving in an erratic fashion prior to the accident?"

"He was going fast."

"But not weaving?"

"I don't think so."

"Did he use his horn?"

"No."

"Any debris in the street—tree limbs, garbage cans?"

"No."

"What about cats or dogs?"

"No."

Rizzo jotted a few notes and capped his pen. He said thanks, that was all he needed. Draining the last of his coffee, he stood to leave. "Oh," he said. "Long as I'm here, would it be okay if I talked to Sara?"

Now it all made sense, why he'd stopped by instead of just calling. There was no way to put him off that wouldn't have looked like I was hiding something. Speechless, I turned to Liz. She was the one who saved the day.

"I'm sorry, Detective," she said, lowering her voice. "We feel like Sara's been through enough. As it is, we've got her seeing a therapist."

The detective nodded in an understanding way. He could appreciate how we felt, he said—he had a daughter too, lived with her mom down the shore. "But Sara might have seen something important, without even realizing it."

Liz nodded back in her own understanding way, assuring him that of course we'd call if Sara mentioned anything. Then she handed him his umbrella. Seeing that he wasn't getting anywhere, the detective forced a smile. "Good enough for me." Then he glanced toward the top of the stairs. I turned to see that Sara had been spying on us. "Keep up the good work, Junior Detective," he said.

"Why can't I talk to him?" Sara said, after he was gone.

Liz and I looked at each other. Who knew how long she'd been up there or what she'd heard?

"Because," Liz said, "he wants to ask you questions about the accident, and we don't think that's a six-year-old's job."

"But what if I want to?"

"Sorry, honey," I said. "It's not up to you."

Rizzo's car was still out front, an unmarked black sedan. He'd gone across the street to secure a corner of the tarp that had blown loose. Seeing him out there in the rain fussing over the memorial gave me a bad feeling. After he left, I went back down to the basement. I had the shop vac going when I noticed Liz standing there with a hand on her hip.

"Well?" she said, when I turned the vac off. "Want to tell me what really happened?"

Liz and I met playing buck-a-trick, buck-a-bump dorm Euchre during our freshman year at Case Western—a pilot's son from Covington who liked to bluff, and a full partner's daughter from the Main Line who would take a bluff—if it fooled her and she lost the trick—as a personal offense. By the end of the second semester, we were sleeping together and done with Euchre, which had gotten too cutthroat between us.

Now, facing her in the glare of the basement's bare bulbs, I knew it was time to put at least some of my cards on the table. And so I told her a percentage of the truth, enough of it for her to understand why I didn't want Sara talking to the detective. I didn't mention trying to scare Juwan, or having been scared *by* him. I just said I'd started to turn in front of him before I realized how fast he was going. Liz bit her lip, studying me, and I knew what a stranger I must have seemed to her then. We'd known each other for eighteen years and been married for ten. She shouldn't have had to wonder whether she could trust me about something so important.

"So you're saying the accident *was* your fault?"

"Probably," I said. "I'm sorry, I should have told you."

"Why didn't you?"

"I was freaked out. I didn't want to believe it."

"Does Sara know?"

"I don't think so."

"Damn it, Glen." She crossed her arms and stared down at the puddle she was standing in. "But he was driving like a maniac, right?"

I nodded.

"And if he hadn't been, he wouldn't have crashed."

"Maybe not."

"Definitely not," she said. "He would have stopped, or just slowed down. So you can't really say it was your fault. You might have been *involved*, but that's not the same. You were just minding your own business. He was the one breaking the law. He caused the accident."

Hearing her say so almost made it sound true.

"But it's good you didn't tell the police," she went on, not waiting for me to agree. "We could still get sued."

I said regardless of whose fault it was, they'd have a hard time proving anything.

"So? They don't have to."

She was right, of course. Her father had been a lawyer, and he'd encouraged us to sue the guy who hit us in Cleveland. "You wouldn't have to prove the guy ran the light," he said, "just that he probably did." It came down to standards of evidence. In a criminal suit, you had to be guilty beyond a reasonable doubt, whereas in a civil suit, all it took was a preponderance of evidence. He compared it to a football game—a criminal conviction would require getting the ball to the one-yard line; a civil conviction would only require getting it past the fifty. "And as far as a jury's concerned," he'd said, nodding at Liz's taut belly, "you're already there."

Liz didn't feel like going out, so we canceled our plans with Lacy's family and ordered Chinese instead.

"No fair," Sara said.

"Sorry, honey," Liz said. "Mom's tired."

She didn't have much to say at dinner, just sat there watching Sara eat her egg drop soup, probably wishing her dad were still around to offer some advice. Afterwards, I sent Sara up to brush her teeth and started to apologize again, but Liz cut me off.

"Are you sure nobody saw what happened?"

"They canvassed the street looking for witnesses."

"You should have told him there was a cat," she said. "That would have been perfect: he swerved to miss a cat."

She went to bed early and slept with Sara again—just in case, she said. I arranged a row of empty soda cans next to the sofa to wake me if I sleepwalked, then lay there in the dark listening for Tawana's car. I wondered if Liz really believed what she'd said about the accident being Juwan's fault, or if that was just her way of circling the wagons. For that matter, had she really believed *me*? Surely the thought that I might still be lying had crossed her mind. Maybe it was a case of her not wanting to know more. Maybe we'd already entered into an unspoken agreement where she wouldn't ask and I wouldn't tell. Of course, the problem with an unspoken agreement is that you can never be sure it really exists.

In the morning, to make amends, I told Liz I'd go to the funeral. I still thought it was a bizarre idea. And perverse on Liz's part. She could talk all she wanted about how the funeral might help Sara, but it didn't ring true, didn't sound like the person who'd cover Sara's eyes just to keep her from seeing a dead bird on the sidewalk. I thought again that she must be doing it to punish me, whether she realized it or not, and here I was, keeping up my end of our unspoken agreement, willing to accept.

"Maybe you're right," I said. "Maybe it'll do her some good."

"I know you don't want to go. I don't blame you."

"I'll be fine."

On the way to the cemetery, Sara started to get anxious. Would we see Juwan's body? she asked. Was it okay if she cried? Was it okay if she didn't? I was surprised, though, at how matter-of-fact she was about death. I figured she just didn't get it. I kept waiting for the light to go on, for her to ask me what I'd asked my dad after my grandmother's funeral: what was the point of anything if we were all just going to die? I had no answer beyond the one I'd been given—the people you love are the point.

The cemetery was the one we passed driving to and from school, near the intersection where we'd seen the Suburban guy—a coincidence that didn't really hit me until later. We followed a long line of cars to a grove shaded by evergreens among rows of pale headstones. There were folding chairs set up under a canopy next to the grave. I had worried we'd stick out, the white strangers at a black funeral, but it was a mixed crowd, and big enough that no one gave us a second look. Still, our being there felt all wrong. We were interlopers, gawkers, tourists. We should have been at the movies or carving a pumpkin, something to take our minds *off* the funeral.

The ground was soft from rain. We stood at the edge of the gathering. Sara was whispering her questions now: Would Juwan go to heaven after the funeral? Was he already there? Was heaven in outer space? How long would it take a rocket to get there?

"I don't know, sweetie," I said. "I wish I did."

Liz nudged me. I looked up. Rizzo was standing twenty feet away from us, alone in a dark suit, looking tired and solemn. He'd spotted us, too, and I was afraid he'd come over, but he just gave a nod. Sara asked if she could go say hello.

"Not now," I said. "It's getting ready to start."

"Do you think he always goes to the funerals?" Liz said softly.

The crowd got quiet as the pastor took his place beside the grave. He was a burly, white-haired man with a voice you didn't have to strain to hear.

"For men are not cast off by the Lord forever," he began. "Though he brings grief, he will show compassion, so great is his unfailing love. For he does not willingly bring affliction or grief to the children of men." He looked up from his Bible. "Today we are gathered here to mourn the passing of one such child. Please join me in prayer."

Sara prayed. I pretended to pray but was watching Tawana over the bowed heads. She was seated under the canopy, her eyes hidden by the brim of her hat. There was a dignified-looking man next to her in a black suit—Juwan's father, I assumed. They didn't comfort one another. They just sat there shoulder to fallen shoulder, looking like the bleakest two people in the world.

While I was watching Tawana, Liz was watching me. I could feel her sidelong glance, as surely as I'd been feeling Rizzo's eyes on us. I wondered if she were seeing me in a new light, standing there surrounded by all the misery I'd caused. I could understand how that might change the way you felt about someone.

I put my arm around her, and she let me keep it there. We stood that way as the pastor quoted more Scripture. He talked about Juwan, whom he'd known personally—what a faithful son he'd been, what a good student, what a cutup. A few of Juwan's friends spoke too, telling funny stories that made people cry, and then there was singing. After a hymn called "My Faith Has Found a Resting Place" ("I trust the ever living One / His wounds for me shall plead"), the pastor closed by inviting people to place roses on top of the casket. There was a basket of them near the grave. Sara wanted to do it, so we got in line. Girls were hugging each other and crying. Boys in blue blazers shuffled along with their hands in their pockets, casting glances at the grave. I've never fainted in my life, but as we got closer, I felt my head getting light. Inside that box, laid out flat, was a boy who was never coming out.

I lifted Sara to lay her flower on the casket. Juwan's parents were just a few yards away. I avoided looking at Tawana until we were clear of the canopy. People were coming up to her now, offering condolences, but her eyes were like an empty stretch of road. She was no more there than Juwan was.

The next morning, Sara asked me to take a different route to school, one that didn't go past the cemetery.

"So he just stays there under the ground forever, all by himself?"

"It's not really him," I said. "Just his body. But we don't ever have to drive by there again if you don't want to."

I had to park three blocks away from school, near the train underpass. When we came up the hill, students were waiting to cross the street as a school bus tried to squeeze past the cars that were parked between the corner and the sign that read NO PARKING FROM HERE TO CORNER. Somebody honked. Standing in the crosswalk, Warren just smiled.

"I'm learning the limits of my authority," he said. Then he called after me, asking if I'd changed my mind.

Sara wanted to know what he was talking about, so I told her.

"Do it, Dad," she said. "You know so much about traffic. You'd be the best crossing guard ever."

She lobbied me all the way across the school yard and up the stairs to her classroom.

"All right," I said finally, seduced, as I'd been so many times, by the prospect of her being proud of me. "Fine."

On the way out, I stopped by Warren's office and said I'd take the morning shift. He gave me a crash course right there at his desk, then said he'd send a link to an online training video.

"It's not such a bad job if you can manage not to take things personally," he said.

*   *   *

That night Liz was an hour late getting home, and when Sara and I met her at the station, she was beat.

"Could we just go sit down somewhere?" she said.

There was a chill in the air. We stopped for coffee and hot cocoa, then headed to the little park across from the train station. On the way, Sara told her I was going to be the new school crossing guard.

"My husband, the Good Samaritan," she said. "Can they sue a crossing guard if a kid gets hurt?"

I think she was only half kidding. Seeing Rizzo at the funeral had her even more worried than before. "It's like he's taking Juwan's side," she'd said. "You know, you and Sara could have been killed, too."

We sat on a bench while Sara ran off to play with Kate, a girl she knew from summer day camp. In between sips of coffee, Liz asked what time I'd have to be at school. I put a finger to my head and pretended to shoot. I was supposed to be there at 8:45, which meant less morning time for her and Sara.

"My mistake. I'll switch to afternoons."

Sara and Kate were marching through a water fountain that had been turned off for the season. Sighing, Liz reached for my hand without taking her eyes off the girls. She said she'd been thinking about the funeral a lot, that if she were ever standing in Tawana's shoes, the last thing she'd want was regrets about not spending enough time with Sara.

"Look at her," she said. "She's not going to be like this forever, and I'm missing it."

"You're the best mom I know," I said. "And you're not missing any more than any other mom who gets off that train."

"I don't care. It's not enough."

Before Sara was born, we'd decided that the path to a sane life was for one of us to stay at home, so I'd quit the accounting firm where I worked in the business tax division and gone into business for myself. Our intention was to trade places at some point, but Liz's career took off, and by the time we got to New Jersey, what we had was an unfair, half-sane life: I got to work at home and spend afternoons with Sara; Liz got a full-time job and an hour-long commute, plus the pressure of being chief breadwinner. It's true that she could have quit and done something else, part-time, or closer to home. I could have gotten a regular job again, with benefits. We could have moved somewhere cheaper, where we'd be able to get by on a tax accountant's salary. So far, though, she hadn't been able to bring herself to give up her job, and neither of us was in a hurry to make do with less.

Now she was telling me she liked the idea of being an independent consultant. Of all the possibilities we'd considered, that was the one she kept coming back to.

"Then quit," I said. "We'll make it work."

"You always make it sound so easy."

Over by the fountain, Sara and Kate had stopped to see Kate's baby sister. Kate's mom was pushing the stroller back and forth. Liz left me sitting there and walked over for a look.

"You must like being a big sister," she said to Kate.

Kate smiled. She was letting the baby squeeze her finger. When her mom said it was okay for Sara to do the same, Sara reached into the stroller, but cautiously, like she was testing hot water.

"Can you believe *you* used to be that small?" Liz said.

As the baby's hand closed around Sara's finger, she shook her head.

"I know," Liz said. "Me, neither."

While I manned the intersection the next morning, Sara stood at the school yard's wrought-iron fence, calling out to her friends as they arrived, "Hey, look, it's my dad!" I couldn't seem to get the hang of it, though. The training video, which I'd watched three times, said to use voice commands for pedestrians and hand signals for traffic. My impulse was to use both, all the time, and I kept forgetting to lower the stop sign. The kids from the high school didn't help, crossing the streets everywhere *except* at the crosswalks.

A little before nine, Sara was on her way into the building with her classmates, waving, when a black SUV started up the hill. At first, I didn't even register the flared fenders. It wasn't until I saw the four wheels in back that it dawned on me—another one of those unexpected second chances, like seeing Juwan again. This time I wouldn't get carried away. I knew just what to do. I stepped into the street and held up the sign, hoping he wouldn't recognize me. As he looked from side to side, trying to figure out why I'd stopped him, I memorized his license plate and the address of an auto body shop advertised on his door.

Fifteen minutes later, I was on my way to Derek's Custom Auto Body. The address was in Orange, along one of the routes we took to school. If that was where he worked, and if he'd been headed to work from his home, his commute overlapped part of ours, only in reverse. My plan was to call the police with an anonymous tip once I made sure he was there. I'd decided not to file a complaint; I didn't want him finding out my name, and I didn't want the police knowing I'd been involved in another traffic incident on the day Juwan was killed.

The shop was just south of the cemetery, between a shuttered Delta station and a ragtag row of houses set close to the curb. I parked around the corner on the off chance he might recognize the station wagon. Several vehicles were out front, including the Suburban. Several more, in various states of repair, were visible inside the garage. There was also a small showroom with a plate glass window. A wall of wheel covers rose behind the counter where the Suburban guy stood talking to a customer.

On the drive over, an idea had begun to take hold of me, slowly, like a drop of oil pooling in a puddle: My run-in with the Suburban guy was no more a mere footnote to the accident than the accident itself was an isolated, out-of-the-blue event. On the contrary, it had been the culmination of that whole afternoon, in which A led to B led to C. Things had started with me flipping off the cop and ended with me cutting the wheel. In between was this guy. If it hadn't been for him, maybe I wouldn't have overreacted to Juwan. Maybe everything would have turned out differently. In any case, it was preposterous that *I* had ended up being the only one in trouble with the police. Wasn't threatening someone with a gun just as bad as threatening someone with a car? And didn't it count for anything that his actions had been premeditated and mine had not?

I was rehearsing what I'd say to the police when I noticed a pay phone on the corner where the gas station used to be. I decided to use it instead of my cell phone, so my number wouldn't show up on caller ID. I got out and crossed the street. The customer was leaving the body shop. Lighting a cigar, the Suburban guy opened a newspaper on the counter. I dialed 911 and told the dispatcher I had an anonymous tip. When she realized I was talking about something that had happened the week before, she told me to call the department's nonemergency number.

"That or Crimestoppers," she said.

There was no phone book, so I dialed information and asked the operator to connect me. While I was waiting, the Suburban guy closed the paper and made his way into the garage.

"Essex County Crimestoppers," a voice said. "Sergeant Carrera speaking."

"I don't have to give my name, right?"

"No, sir. At no point will I ask your name."

The sergeant said I'd be assigned a code number, which I could then use to call back for updates on the case and to collect my reward if my information led to an arrest. I said I wasn't after a reward, I just wanted to report someone, and proceeded to tell him what had happened, minus the part about flipping off the cop. I told him the reason I was calling anonymously was that I wanted to protect my family. He said he understood.

"But a case like this," he said, "where there's no crime in progress, where it's just going to be your word against his, I'm sorry—you've got to file a complaint before we can do anything."

"Then couldn't you just leave me out of it altogether? Get him for an illegal handgun?"

"You know it's illegal?"

I'd been hoping so, just as I'd been hoping they'd find drugs if they searched the Suburban. "Can't you run a check?"

"Sir, we don't even have a name."

"I could get it."

"Look," he said, "we can't just show up and search the guy without probable cause. We'd still need a complaint."

I told him I'd think it over and hung up. The Suburban guy was talking to a mechanic in the garage. Possibly there

was a business card with his name on it back at the register.
But it still wasn't worth filing a complaint. He hadn't cared
that there was a child in the car when he'd shown me his
gun. It was hard to imagine him having any compunction
about coming after me or my family. What was to stop him
from driving by the house one night, shooting it up?

By now he'd noticed me at the pay phone, watching him.
He stopped talking to the mechanic and fixed me with a
stare. He didn't seem to recognize me, though. I returned
his stare long enough to convince myself I wasn't afraid of
him, and then I went home.

When I picked Sara up, I told Warren I needed to switch to
the afternoon, like I'd promised Liz; the fringe benefit was
that I probably wouldn't be crossing paths with the Suburban guy at that hour. I made sure not to drive past his shop
on the way home. I didn't drive past the cemetery, either.

Sara asked why I'd changed shifts.

"So we'll have more time with Mom in the morning," I
said.

"Is she going to quit her job?"

Liz hadn't said anything else about quitting to me. "Did
she tell you she was?"

"No. She just asked me would I like it if she worked at
home."

"Would you?"

"I think you both should."

I said that would be great, but one of us needed a regular job. I was starting to explain health insurance when she interrupted.

"Hey, isn't that the mom from the funeral?"

We'd just passed a woman on the sidewalk that led into our neighborhood. I slowed down and looked back, a knot already forming in my stomach. After the funeral, I'd been hoping never to see Tawana again, but here she was, in jeans and a too-big sweater that might have been Juwan's, carrying a shovel.

"Sweetie," I said. "I think you're right."

And for a split second, before I realized Tawana must have been headed for the memorial, I thought she was coming for *me*.

"Why does she have an axe?" Sara said.

"I think it was a shovel," I said, reminding myself that Tawana had no reason to blame me.

"Dad, I'm not stupid. It was an axe."

I circled the block and came up behind Tawana again. It was an axe. She was holding it near the blade, its long wooden handle swinging at her side. She looked determined to get wherever it was she was going. It occurred to me that if she tried to hurt herself, there was no one else around to intervene. I put the window down.

"Excuse me," I said. "Are you all right?"

She kept walking. I couldn't tell if she even knew we were there. How far had she come? I wondered. Why was she on foot? Why hadn't anyone stopped her? At that point, I decided the best thing to do was call the police, and this time I wasn't ashamed of the impulse. I sped up, put the car in the garage, and took Sara inside. As I was closing the curtains in her room, she asked what was going on. I said I wasn't sure, but I wanted her to stay away from the window. Then I parted the blinds and waited. A couple of minutes passed. Tawana came around the corner, walking with more purpose now, carrying the axe with two hands. She crossed the street into Clarice's yard. When she reached the tree, she didn't hesitate. She planted her feet, drew back, and swung with all her might. There was a dull thud. A crow lifted off from the branches above her. She swung so hard she fell, knocking over some flowers. The axe was lodged in the tree. At first it wouldn't budge. She had to choke up and use both hands to loosen the blade. As soon as it was free, she took another swing. She swung as if she intended to fell the tree with one blow, as if her life depended on it. I took out my phone.

"She's trying to kill Sicky!" Sara cried. "Stop it!"

I found her banging on the bathroom window, trying to get Tawana's attention. I pulled her away, telling her I'd take care of it, and hurried downstairs. Tawana ignored me as I crossed the street. There were grass stains on her knees, leaves stuck to her sweater. Her hair, burnt orange in the afternoon light, was unkempt. The tree trunk was nicked with axe marks. Now that I was out there, I wished I'd gone ahead and called the police first. I wasn't worried about the axe so much as simply having to face her.

"Ms. Richards?"

As I approached her, she drew back and took another swing, her eyes so full of tears I don't know how she could see what she was doing. Down at the corner, a woman pushing a stroller turned around and went back the way she'd come. On the next swing, the axe got stuck again. That's when Sara's voice reached us. She was standing just outside our front door, begging Tawana to stop. Tawana didn't bother trying to free the axe. She let go of the handle and looked at Sara and then me, her chest rising and falling.

"Your daughter," she said.

I nodded.

"She doesn't want me to hurt the tree."

"Come on," I said, hoping to get her away from the axe. "Come inside."

She righted the bouquet she'd knocked over, then brushed leaves from her sweater. "I'm not crazy," she said. "I know the tree didn't kill him. I just can't stand the sight of it."

"Me, neither."

She followed me back across the street. Sara was standing on the porch, looking at Tawana as if she were on fire.

"It's just a few scratches," I said to Sara. "No big deal."

Tawana took a deep breath and let it out. "I'm sorry, baby. Sometimes grown-ups get upset and do things they shouldn't."

Sara nodded, staring at her feet now.

"Why don't you go up to your room," I said.

Tawana waited until Sara was gone before she covered her mouth and started to cry. I have never felt like more of a monster than I did at that moment, too shamed with guilt to even put a hand on her shoulder. I asked if she wanted to sit down. She went to the sofa. I got a box of tissues and set it on the coffee table in front of her. She had her face in her hands.

"I'm Glen," I said. "I saw the whole thing."

"I know who you are, Mr. Bauer," she said, wiping her eyes. "Your neighbor told me. You thought they gave up on him too soon. You were the only one who spoke up."

She was looking at me as if I might be able to tell her something about her son's death that no one else knew. I could no more meet her eyes than I could have gazed into the sun.

"They said he was already dead."

She sighed. "And were they white? The medics?"

"Yes." I supposed, in her shoes, I might have asked the same question.

"I just don't see how they can quit before they even get him to the hospital."

"I'm sorry," I said. "I'm so sorry."

She shook her head. "I should be apologizing to *you*. They told me he could have hit you instead of the tree. But you know what my first thought was? Not 'Oh Lord, what if he'd hurt someone?' It was 'Why *him*? Why not *them* instead?'" She closed her hand on the tissue and bit her lip. "I'm a *Christian*, Mr. Bauer."

I took a step toward her but couldn't go any farther. I

asked if she wanted me to call someone, or give her a ride. She didn't seem to hear me.

"It was my car," she said. "He wasn't supposed to be driving it."

She was looking out the window. There were two police cruisers out front. Both officers, a man and a woman, were talking to Clarice. Tawana stood and smoothed her sweater. Then she walked out the door and met the female officer as she was coming up the steps. They seemed to know each other. The officer gave me a nod. Tawana opened the door and got into the police car by herself. Clarice was in her bathrobe again, watching from the porch. She didn't come out to check on the tree until after they were gone.

Maybe when you read this you'll wonder why I didn't just do the right thing and tell her the truth. Believe me, it's not like the idea hadn't crossed my mind. But having a clearer conscience wasn't worth getting us sued and maybe going to jail. When I thought about what my confessing would do to you and your mom, that was all the reason I needed to keep quiet.

And yet. The point here is to be completely honest. I have to admit that even without you, I'd probably still have found an excuse to keep covering up what I'd done. I wanted to do right, but the price was just too high.

Liz had barely gotten into the car that night when Sara announced that Juwan's mom had tried to chop down the tree.

"With an *axe*," she said. "But Dad saved Sicky. He got her to come inside."

"Into our house?" Liz looked at me like I was crazy. I shook my head and explained what happened, and she calmed down once she realized Tawana hadn't brought the axe inside.

"At least she didn't hurt herself," she said.

"The tree's not hurt either," Sara said. "Not too bad. Dad let me put some more gauze on even though the flowers are still there."

It wasn't until later, when Liz and I were alone in the kitchen, that she asked if Tawana and I had talked about the accident. I told her what Tawana had said about me being the only one who'd spoken up for Juwan and how terrible that made me feel.

"It wasn't your fault, Glen. Having a guilty conscience isn't the same as being guilty."

I had a pot roast going in the slow cooker, the first decent meal we'd had since the accident. I checked to see if the potatoes were done.

"And if there's ever a lawsuit," she said, "maybe what you did today will count for something."

"I honestly don't think she cares about that."

Liz held a plate while I served. "She will. That's what people do. Your child gets killed in an accident, sooner or later you hire a lawyer to make sure somebody pays."

I told her Clarice had said Tawana's ex was a radiologist. She had a big house in the historic district. She'd already replaced the Jaguar with a BMW.

"You know as well as I do," Liz said, "it's not about the money. It's about not being able to do anything else."

After the accident in Cleveland, we'd have been happy to settle with the insurance company and be done with it, but the guy who hit us didn't have insurance, and for us to collect on our uninsured motorist coverage, we would have had to sue him first, make him pay what he could. We were in a tough spot. Liz was due in two months, and we didn't want the hassle.

Liz's dad offered to help, but we went to see the guy instead, to see if he wanted to settle out of court. We were looking for just enough money to replace the car and cover the emergency room. The guy didn't have it, though. He was renting a little two-bedroom place out in Euclid with his wife and kids. The delivery truck was all he owned, and he couldn't even afford to get the bumper fixed. So we let it go.

But it's not like Liz and I were saints. We never talked about it, never said the words, but it was always there between us: if there had been a problem when Sara was born—anything even remotely attributable to the accident—we would have sued him into the ground.

*   *   *

On Thursday, while Sara was at school, I met with a client from the neighborhood, a stockbroker named Carlos who was getting audited. I gave him my standard pep talk. I said some people thought my job was to help clients get away with as much as they could, but the way I saw it, I served them best when they paid exactly what they owed—not a penny more, not a penny less. I would run the numbers every which way, I'd dig up all the tax breaks I could find, I'd turn the code inside out, but in the end, everything had to be legit. Otherwise you risked paying a lot more later.

"So don't worry," I told him. "You've already paid what you owed."

Back home, going over Carlos's returns, I was happy to lose myself in the numbers for a while, but at some point my screen saver kicked in, and I found myself watching a slide show: Sara playing tee-ball, Sara learning to ride her bike, Sara touching noses with Chairman Meow. It was impossible not to think of Tawana and what it would be like to look at those pictures knowing I'd never see Sara again.

I put on a sweatshirt and went outside. The front yard was covered in leaves. I'd been avoiding raking because I didn't want to be out there when one of Juwan's friends stopped by, which they'd continued doing since the funeral. But I figured I was safe until school let out. I unfolded a tarp, the one I'd covered the memorial with, and started raking. As I was dragging a load of leaves to the curb, a black sedan came down the street. I thought to duck behind the hedge a moment too late. Rizzo parked and got out, holding a manila folder.

"Mr. Bauer," he said. "Spare a minute?"

I propped the rake against a tree and met him on the sidewalk with what was becoming a familiar sense of dread. I figured he was there about Sara again, maybe hoping I'd changed my mind since the funeral. I steeled myself to tell him I hadn't.

"Heard you had a little scene here," he said, glancing over at the sycamore. The gauze had started to sag, revealing the axe marks. "As if that funeral wasn't hard enough."

"Sara asked us to take her," I said, not wanting him to think I'd gone out of guilt but probably giving him that impression anyway, blurting out an excuse like that. "She's still trying to get her head around the fact that he's gone."

"Poor kid," he said. "Look, never mind about me talking to her. I think we've got what we need. Turns out the guy was on his phone. So with the speeding and maybe alcohol too—it should be an open-and-shut case."

I nodded, trying to play it cool. "So that's it?"

"Yeah, depending on the autopsy."

I felt as if my knees might buckle, the relief was so huge. I asked if they'd ever found out where Juwan had been in such a hurry to get to.

Rizzo said they weren't sure. "But we know where he was coming from. He'd just left his girlfriend's house."

"Were they fighting?"

"Apparently the opposite," he said. "And drinking. His friends say he wasn't much of a drinker, though. He was probably a lot worse off than he realized." He noticed me looking at the folder and smiled like I'd caught him at something. "I did want to ask you about these, though," he said, pulling out a couple of eight-by-tens. "My ex, she tells me I have an inability to leave well enough alone." They were photographs of the crash scene. He tapped one of them. "Right here. It looks like you overshot your driveway a little. Then I remembered, when the tow truck got here, I think you had to back up so you could pull in. Am I right?"

My scalp tightened as I began to see what he was getting at: if I'd been waiting for Juwan to pass so I could pull into my driveway, why would I have overshot it? He'd probably figured out that I'd started to turn, then didn't, then had to keep going to get back into my lane. I looked from one photo to the other, trying not to panic.

"Maybe it's the angle."

He shook his head. "We got it from a couple angles. See?"

I studied the photos some more. A breeze was whisking leaves off the tarp, but I was burning up inside my sweatshirt, ready to melt. I couldn't decide which would be worse—pleading ignorance or admitting I might have started to turn. I was still trying to make up my mind, on the verge of what felt like surrender, when it occurred to me that the explanation I needed was already there, just waiting for me, in the statement I'd given at the station.

"Oh," I said. "I remember. My foot came off the brake when I reached for Sara." I handed the pictures back to him. "The car started to roll, and I realized it was still in gear, that I needed to put it in park."

"But why did you cut the wheel?"

"What do you mean?"

"Your front tires—they're turned toward the curb. Away from your driveway."

"I don't know. I guess I still had a hand on the wheel when I reached for her." I mimed the action of holding the steering wheel with my left hand, turning it as I reached back with my right. "I must have turned it without meaning to."

Instead of the stony disbelief I was expecting, Rizzo said, "Makes sense."

I'd managed to regain my composure, but the fact that he once again seemed so willing to take me at my word was starting to worry me. A guilty conscience can be tricky that way: knowing I was lying made it hard to believe anyone else could believe me. I couldn't help thinking he was just biding his time, lulling me, waiting for me to drop my guard.

He slid the photos back into the folder and thanked me. I said I was sorry I hadn't been more help.

"Anything I can cross off my list, that's a help." His car window was open. He tossed the folder onto the seat.

"Funny thing about that funeral," he said. "I'm standing there, checking things out, and I realize I'm looking at the county highway building. On Thomas Boulevard, right across from the cemetery? Our crime scene garage is in there. That's where we have his car." He took his keys out, spun them on his finger. "I mean, of all the places he could have been buried, he's right across the street from his car. No getting away from it, I guess."

Driving to pick up Sara that afternoon, I looked for the place Rizzo was talking about. I had to see it for myself. It was half a block down from where I'd flipped off the cop, a long brick building with a fenced parking lot, two metal garage doors, and a sign that read GOD BLESS AMERICA. All of the ground-floor windows had been sealed off or fitted with bars.

I didn't stop to talk with the other parents when I got to school. I went straight to the office, picked up my gear, and set the orange cones in the no-parking zones. I was already working the crosswalks by the time Sara's class was dismissed. She came over to the fence to say hi, then went to play with Lacy.

Warren had warned me that afternoons were more hectic than mornings. The high school let out at the same time as Sara's school. Kids were everywhere, on bikes and skateboards, darting from between cars, crossing the street in groups. At the pizza place on the corner, the line was out the door, spilling off the sidewalk. There were school buses and parents waiting for parking spots and a convoy of dusty cement trucks from who knew where. I should have been concentrating on making sure nobody got run over, but I couldn't stop thinking about the Jaguar inside that building, picturing a police mechanic breaking it down piece by piece.

No getting away from it, Rizzo had said. As if he knew how my mistakes had converged in that no-man's-land along Thomas Boulevard, a coincidence of geography I couldn't help being spooked by, looking for meaning where there was none, feeling like the universe itself had it in for me.

When we got home, I called Liz to tell her Rizzo no longer needed to talk to Sara because it was an open-and-shut case now—Juwan had been on his cell phone. She was more suspicious than relieved.

"He stopped by for that? Why didn't he just call?"

"He wanted to ask me about some photos too. No big deal."

"What photos?"

I took a deep breath and told her the rest, even though I knew she wouldn't like it. Then I counted to five-one-thousand, the way you count seconds between lightning and thunder.

"No big deal?" she said. "Are you kidding me, Glen? He pretty much has it figured out. He knows you started to turn."

"He doesn't know anything. I told him my foot came off the brake when I reached for Sara."

"And let me guess," she said. "You think he believed you."

The next morning, I got a call from an attorney in East Orange. I was in the kitchen packing Sara's lunch, and Liz was upstairs prodding her to get dressed for school. We picked up at the same time, and I asked her to stay on, knowing she'd want to hear for herself whatever he had to say.

The attorney explained that he'd been engaged by Tawana Richards to explore the possibility of a wrongful death action involving her son. He was wondering if I might stop by his office to talk about the accident.

"I understand you and your daughter were the only witnesses," he said.

"She was with me," I told him, "but I'm the only one who saw what happened."

I knew I wasn't under any obligation to talk to him, but I also knew it would look bad if I didn't. I agreed to meet with him the following week. As I hung up, Liz came into the kitchen in a camisole and flannel pajama pants, holding the phone to her chest.

"See?" she said, her voice barely a whisper.

I put my arms around her and pointed out that I wasn't being deposed, that there wasn't even a lawsuit—this was just an informal thing, what the lawyer had called prelitigation discovery. "It's a fishing expedition. It's where he finds out there's no one to sue."

She turned away and spread her hands on the countertop, as if all her strength were needed to keep it in place. "Jesus, Glen," she said. "We could lose everything."

As soon as she got to work, Liz emailed me the name of an attorney that a friend of hers in the bank's legal department had recommended. She phoned later, that afternoon, to see if I'd followed up. I was in the waiting room at Kim Lee's office, trying again to listen through the door as Sara told her about the funeral, Tawana, the axe. I stepped out into the hallway and told Liz I didn't want a lawyer, that it would just make me look guilty. There was more to it than that, though. Getting a lawyer would have *felt* like admitting my guilt to the world, and at that point, I could hardly admit it to myself.

"I'd rather wait until there's actually a lawsuit," I said. "Which there won't be."

"Just call her, honey. Can't you do that for me?"

I said I was sorry, but I really didn't think hooking up with a lawyer was a good idea.

She gave an exasperated sigh. "Okay, we obviously can't have this conversation now. Get a sitter for tonight, all right?"

We went straight from the train station to the Indian restaurant in Maplewood. Liz had brought a bottle of wine from the city. No sooner had we sat down and gotten it poured than she picked up where she'd left off, wanting to know how I could be so mulish.

"You don't go see a lawyer unless you've got a lawyer," she said.

"I already told you. I'll get one if I need one."

"If you need one?" She reached across the table for my wrist. "That boy is dead, Glen. Do you really think that's the end of it, that there aren't going to be consequences? It doesn't matter if he got himself killed. You were still in-volved, and now Rizzo knows it."

The waiter came over. Neither of us was hungry, but I ordered some nan and samosas. Once we were alone again, Liz poured more wine and started speculating about how I'd fare in criminal court (pretty well) versus civil court (not well at all). I tried changing the subject. I told her Kim Lee wanted to keep seeing Sara. I asked if she'd given any more thought to quitting her job. I said I'd heard about a posi-tion at a firm in Hoboken that I could apply for. She was still obsessing over the possibility of a lawsuit, though. It was a lose-lose, she said: they take you for everything you've got, or you spend everything you've got trying to stop them. Good-bye house, good-bye savings, good-bye college. She said she knew what her dad would say.

"He'd tell me to get out while I can. If you won't even protect yourself, why should Sara and I suffer too?"

After we got home and put Sara to bed, Liz poured another glass of wine, took it into the living room, and lit a fire in the fireplace. At midnight, I was still waiting for her to come to bed. I didn't agree with what she'd said at the restaurant. My father-in-law might have been hard-nosed, but he was first and foremost reasonable. If anything, he'd have advised her not to lose her head.

Twice Liz came upstairs to look in on Sara, passing our bedroom without a word. At 1 a.m., I stood at the window watching her come back from the woodpile with an armful of logs. Later, I could hear her opening the metal fireplace curtain to put another one on.

I came down at dawn, before Sara woke up. Liz was asleep on the sofa. Her laptop was on the coffee table, next to a glass and a half-empty bottle of wine. The embers in the fireplace were still glowing. I got some aspirin and water. She sat up, took the pills, and drank the whole glass.

"I'll call the lawyer," I said. "I'm not saying I'll take her to the meeting, but I'll talk to her at least."

"Good." Liz pulled a knitted throw around her shoulders and rubbed her eyes. She looked almost as much a mess as Tawana had, sitting in that same spot a few days earlier, but her voice was calm. "That's not going to keep us from getting sued, though."

"Honey, if they sue us, they sue us. That's out of our control."

"Not really. Not if there's a way to separate our assets so they'd just be suing you."

The deliberateness of her logic was making me uneasy. "But there's not, so what's the point?" I closed the fireplace, gathered up the bottle and glasses. "Let's get away for the weekend. If you don't feel like Philly, we could take the train down to Baltimore."

"Glen, listen to me. The statute of limitations on a wrongful death action is two years."

"So?" I left her sitting on the sofa.

She followed me into the kitchen, lowering her voice. "So what if we were apart until then? Until it's safe to get back together."

"Why didn't I think of that?" I turned to her in mock wonder. "A temporary divorce. Sara will love it. Let's go tell her right now."

"Stop it, Glen."

"No, Liz. You stop."

"But I'm serious."

She did seem serious. Of course, she'd also seemed serious every time she'd vowed to quit her job, stop buying Sara so many doll clothes, or strangle the next loudmouth using a cell phone beside her on the train.

"No, you're not. That's the stupidest thing you've ever said."

Her eyes were surprisingly focused. "Do you have a better idea?"

"Um, yeah. To get a grip on reality. I messed up, Liz—I get it. You've made your point."

I was trying to get the cork back into the bottle. Liz closed her hand over mine until she had my full attention. She reminded me that she was the one who went to an office every day, she was the one who paid the mortgage, she was the one saving for college and our retirement.

"Great. Is that what this is about?"

"It's about Sara," she said. "Her future. I've worked hard to give her a good one—we both have—and I'm going to make sure she gets it."

By the time Sara came downstairs, Liz was in bed. I told Sara she wasn't feeling well again. Sara wanted to make her a get-well card.

"And one for Sicky too," she said.

She worked on them in the kitchen while I made pancakes and tried to explain why it wouldn't be appropriate to add Sicky's card to the memorial. All the while, I was trying not to get too wound up over my conversation with Liz. Sometimes she got carried away and said things she didn't mean. It wasn't the real Liz, though, and sooner or later she always cooled down. I got the fire going again, and we ate breakfast in front of the TV. The World Series had started.

We caught the highlights from the previous night's game, which Sara watched with more than her usual mild interest.

"I don't want to be a fairy anymore," she said. "I want to be a baseball player."

It took me a moment to realize she was talking about Halloween. "That's a great idea," I said, glad to have a project. After we ate, we found a pair of her tee-ball pants, used fabric markers to color stirrups on some tube socks, and turned an old T-shirt into a jersey by drawing buttons and piping and CLEVELAND across the front. She already had an Indians cap.

Standing at the mirror, she frowned. "I think I need a real jersey, Dad. And spikes, not sneakers."

I was telling her they probably didn't make metal spikes for six-year-olds when we heard Liz moving around upstairs. It was almost noon. I'd been hoping the extra sleep would improve her outlook, but after she made a big deal over Sara's costume ("Go Tribe!") and the get-well card ("I feel better already"), she started heading back to bed with her laptop.

"Come on, Liz," I said. "Let's get out of the house. We need a pumpkin."

"And a baseball jersey," Sara added.

"You two go," Liz said. "I have some work to do."

I asked Sara to wait for me downstairs and looked over Liz's shoulder at a list of divorce lawyers on the screen. Her plan, she said, was to get on the phone Monday morning and find one who could meet with her as soon as possible.

I said, as calmly as I could, as though this were a perfectly reasonable thing to be discussing, "That's no way to find a good lawyer."

"It would be an uncontested divorce. We wouldn't need good. We'd need fast."

It occurred to me then that she might really be losing it. I closed the door and sat on the bed. I said maybe the two of *us* should go see Kim Lee. "Because honey? Honestly? This is getting crazy. This isn't something a normal person would consider—especially a person with a six-year-old daughter."

She said I was absolutely right—a normal person would sit around hoping she didn't get sued, and then when she did, she'd be screwed. "We're lucky, though. We see it coming. We have time to do something."

"Why don't you ask Sara what she thinks?"

That got her attention. She leaned against the headboard, blinking back tears. "I know this isn't ideal, okay? It fucking sucks. But the alternative is worse. This is the rest of our lives we're talking about. Two years is nothing."

"Honey, what are you doing?" I couldn't believe she was serious, but I was starting to sense that it was dangerous. Even if she was only trying to scare me, or punish me for scaring her, there was a risk that all her talk would make itself come true—and that my reaction, if I let myself go, would only inflame things. I wanted to throw the laptop out the window, but instead I just reminded her that there wasn't even a lawsuit yet. She said if we waited until there was, then obviously it would be too late. I reminded her that we had a boatload of liability coverage. She said the insurance company wouldn't pay if I were convicted of a crime. I pointed out that she herself had said that was unlikely. I said if it would make her feel better, I'd be glad to put everything in her name. She said that wasn't good enough.

"As long as we're married, they can get to it."

Sara and I found pumpkins at a roadside stand and baseball jerseys at the mall. She was adamant about not wanting the Yankees and got a Mets jersey instead. I wondered if her choice had something to do with the Suburban guy's cap but didn't ask. Why remind her of things I was hoping she'd forget?

When we got home, Liz was going through the file cabinet in the office, pulling out papers. I thumbed through the stack—life insurance policies, the deed to the house, bank statements, paperwork on Sara's 529 and our retirement plans.

"Is there anything else going on that I should know about?" I said.

"You mean other than the fact that you've jeopardized everything we've worked so hard for and now you won't do anything about it?"

"So you're not in love with some guy at work? You're not just pissed off at me in general?"

She looked as if she were out of patience.

"I'm not trying to be flip. I just don't understand you."

"The feeling," she said, turning back to the file cabinet, "is mutual."

That's when I told her to make no mistake—if she filed for a divorce, I most certainly would contest it. She'd need a court order to get me out. And of course I'd fight for custody. "So anyhow, we're carving the pumpkin now. Want to take a break and rejoin your family?"

———————

I'm trying not to make your mom out to be the bad guy, but it's hard. I have to keep reminding myself how scared she must have been—not just of what might happen to us, but of me. I'd shaken her faith in my judgment. I'd gone from being the person she could always rely on to a liability, a question mark, a threat.

But for her to plow ahead, knowing what a separation would do to you—even now, that still boggles my mind. It's not as though all she cared about was money. And despite the fact that she could be severe, it's not as though she had a hard heart— far from it. The only thing I can figure is that fear got the best of her, plain and simple. Maybe it had something to do with being a lawyer's daughter, a childhood of legal horror stories at the dinner table—the same way, say, Rizzo's daughter might have grown up with a dark view of human nature.

———————

That night, Liz called her mom to ask if she'd come stay for a while. She told her we'd decided to take some time off from each other.

"Not true," I said, coming out of the bathroom.

"Who's cheating on who?" Helen said, loud enough for me to hear.

I couldn't take it; I went downstairs and got on the other phone. "Helen?" I said. "I was almost involved in a car accident last week. A boy died. Liz is afraid I'll get sued and we'll lose everything, so she wants a divorce. Then she wants to get back together when it's safe."

There was the sound of Helen lighting a cigarette. She was quiet for a long time. I was hoping she'd tell Liz she was out of her mind.

"Well," she said. "That's some plan." Then she said it wasn't her place to judge, of course she'd come if we needed her. She'd been planning to stay with us during tax season anyway, like she always did. "I'll just come earlier."

"You don't need to go along with this," I said. "It's not going to happen."

"Will you get off the phone?" Liz said. "Mom, listen, I'll call you later."

When she hung up, Liz was furious. "What if she tells someone?"

"I hope she tells *everyone*."

"They could make her testify."

I just stared at her. She pressed the heel of her hand to her forehead.

"All right," she said, "that didn't make any sense. But dammit, this has to stay between *us*."

"What about Sara? What are you going to tell her?"

The next morning, Liz called in sick for the first time in two years, then started calling lawyers. She found one out in Livingston who could meet with her at noon, and she was home from his office in time to ride with me to pick up Sara. On the way, she went over the eight grounds for divorce in New Jersey, ticking them off on her fingers: extreme cruelty, adultery, desertion, addiction, institutionalization, imprisonment, deviant sexual conduct. She said the lawyer, Floyd Braun, had recommended extreme cruelty, because it was the easiest.

"It's just a term of art. It doesn't mean anybody was actually cruel."

"Why are you even telling me this crap?" I said. "And I thought there were eight."

"There's also no-fault separation," she said, "but that takes eighteen months."

That night, I got on the computer myself, wanting to find out what I might be in for and what I could do about it. After an hour or so, I was coming to the conclusion that

I'd need a divorce lawyer myself when I happened across an advice column, a lawyer responding to a question about debts and marriage in New Jersey. Referring to a precedent in the state case law, he said that the courts typically didn't hold separated spouses accountable for one another's debts.

Separated, as opposed to divorced.

Reading the column again, it occurred to me that I was going about things all wrong. Fighting wasn't getting me anywhere; it only made Liz dig her heels in. Maybe the best thing to do was play along, ride it out until she came to her senses. In the meantime, I'd be in a better position to keep her from doing any real harm.

I printed out the column. Liz was in bed, circling ads in an apartment finder. "Good-bye, divorce," I said, laying my discovery in her lap. "We could just separate instead." I couldn't believe I was saying it, but I didn't plan on being gone long, just time enough for things to cool off. "We'll make it look like we're planning a no-fault divorce while we wait out the statute of limitations."

She closed the apartment finder and started reading. "And you'd go along with this?"

"It would be easier," I said, "and faster. And a million times less likely to completely ruin Sara's life."

She didn't look convinced. "What happened to a court order and all that?"

I said I didn't want us getting wiped out any more than she did, and I certainly didn't want a divorce. "Do you want to try this or not?"

———————

Up until that day, I'd thought of myself as a man who would never leave his family, and yet that's what I was proposing to do. It's important to me that you understand why.

First, as hard as it was for me to believe, your mom was apparently serious. She's a willful person. And it was a complicated situation; despite what she said, I can't believe the accident was the only thing she was reacting to. I think she must have been mad at me for a while, or disappointed at the way our marriage had turned out. Somehow all of that got tangled up in the decision she was making. So for me, it was come up with plan B or fight her all the way to court.

Second, I felt like I owed her. I was the one who'd gotten us into trouble—or at least potential trouble—and then lied to her about it.

And third, considering what Tawana was going through, who was I to complain about a few weeks apart from my family?

Because that's what I thought it would be—a few weeks. Once I was out of the house and she saw there was no lawsuit coming, she'd realize how foolish she was being, what a terrible mistake she'd made. I was sure it was only a matter of time. I swear to you, sweetie, if I'd thought there were even a chance I'd be gone longer, I never would have left.

———————

In the morning, Liz called Floyd Braun and told him we were considering a no-fault divorce but that she was concerned about potential legal trouble arising from my tax work. She didn't actually say I had shady clients, but that's what it sounded like. She asked if she'd be liable for any judgments against me during the separation period. Braun more or less confirmed what I'd told her. He said a divorce was the only foolproof way, but yes, for all intents and purposes, a separation was just as good in New Jersey.

"But what if the judge decided we hadn't been apart long enough?" she said.

He said that was unlikely, so long as it was clear to the court that we intended to divorce.

After she hung up, she stood at the sink with her hands on her hips, staring out the window at Sara, who was in the backyard waiting for me to drive her to school.

"We can start looking for a place this weekend," she said. "But you heard him. It has to look like we mean it."

We got a sitter for Sara and went to see Braun after work. His office was on the second floor of an old bank building. He was older than I expected, old enough to be in Florida doing nothing but playing golf. Before we sat down, he asked if my lawyer would be joining us. I said I didn't have one because I wouldn't be contesting anything. His thick eyebrows went up.

"It's a good idea to at least talk to someone," he said, "but there's no law that says you have to."

We told him we were leaning toward a no-fault divorce because we thought it would be easier on all of us, especially Sara. He made some notes in longhand on a yellow pad.

"The required separation period is eighteen months," he said, glancing over his glasses. "Basically that means no sleeping under the same roof."

We said we wanted to go ahead and separate our assets as soon as possible. He recommended something called a marital separation agreement, which would go into effect immediately and then be merged with the judicial decree once we filed for divorce. It would cover everything from visitation and child support to property and debt division, health insurance, disposition of the marital home, pension plans, tax issues.

"An MSA is also a good way of demonstrating no reasonable expectation for reconciliation," he said.

On the way home, at Liz's urging, I called Tawana's lawyer and put off our meeting for a week, to buy more time.

The next day was Halloween. Despite the Mets jersey, Sara stuck with her Indians cap, out of loyalty. She was also loaded down with plastic jewelry.

"World Series rings," she said, fanning her hands for us to admire.

It was barely dusk, but the sidewalks were already busy with trick-or-treaters. Sara immediately fell in with twin princesses, sisters she'd met at a neighborhood cookout that summer. Across the street, some other kids had stopped to look at the memorial. I overheard one saying the tree was haunted now.

Not wanting to ruin Halloween, Liz and I had decided to hold off telling Sara I was moving out. More to the point, we hadn't figured out *what* to tell her. We talked it over that night, hanging back as Sara went door to door with her plastic pumpkin, Liz in her annual witch hat, me in my devil horns.

Liz came home early the next night so the three of us would have time for a walk at the county park on South Mountain before dark.

"What about dinner?" Sara said.

"We'll eat later," I said.

As we made our way along a trail to the waterfall, Liz and I began laying out the situation for Sara. We tried to keep it light. We told her I was going to start building up my business in case Liz quit her job, because we'd need the extra money. I'd be working all the time.

"So I've decided to get an apartment," I said. "Nana will stay with us, just like during tax season."

We both knew how lame this was, but it was the best we'd come up with.

"Why do you need an apartment?" Sara said.

"To do more work."

"Are you going to live there?"

"For a while."

"But if it's like tax season, why can't you just work and live at home?"

I said I'd be even busier.

"Can't you be busy at home?"

"Not busy enough."

"But why do you need an apartment to do your work?"

"Same reason Mom goes to an office," I said. "You get more done."

"Then why don't you get an office?"

"That's basically what it'll be, an office I can sleep at."

Sara frowned—she knew double-talk when she heard it. "But I want you to sleep at home."

We were on a flight of stone steps that led to a look-out above the waterfall. We'd been up there before, right after we moved. The steps had been too much for Sara's three-year-old legs, so I'd carried her most of the way. Now I was this close to saying that's it, screw it, I can't go through with this—except I was still convinced I'd be looking at papers for a real divorce the moment I gave up this pretend one. I reminded myself I'd be back home soon, and Sara would eventually forget the whole thing, just like she'd forgotten having ever been on those steps before.

"Race you to the top," I said.

Sara didn't feel like racing, but when we got to the terrace, she let me hold her hand as she balanced on a stone wall next to the path. On the other side, a sheet of rock sloped into a ravine that funneled the river toward the falls. That time of year, it wasn't much of a river, narrow enough to step across in places.

"What a view," Liz said, brightly.

The sun was low, lighting up the trees across the ravine, but Sara was staring at the ground. She asked when I was moving out.

"I'm not moving out. Like I said, I'll just be staying there for a while."

"For how long?"

I said I didn't know, but we'd see each other every day because I'd still be driving her to school. "And you can come over every afternoon. And we can have sleepovers."

She let go of my hand and hopped down onto the rock, poking at a patch of moss. "I thought you were going to be so busy."

"Not too busy to spend time with you."

"What about bedtime?"

"We'll figure it out, sweetie," I said. "Hey, listen to that."

She glanced up from the moss, seeming for the first time to notice the river, the hiss of the falls.

"Let's go see," I said.

"Not too close," Liz said.

The slope wasn't steep. There were bits of broken glass, crushed cans, cigarette butts—a place where teenagers came to drink. Sara started reading the graffiti on the rocks: somebody plus somebody forever, somebody had been there, somebody RIP. Up ahead, the boulder with the most graffiti marked the top of the falls, the point at which the river disappeared in midair. Twenty-five feet below, ripples spread across a pool.

"That's far enough," Liz said.

"But I want to see the waterfall," Sara said. "Isn't that why we came up here?"

I pulled her onto my lap. "We'll see it on the way back, from down there."

"To see it from up here," Liz said, "you'd have to go over it."

Three days after our meeting with Floyd Braun, the mail carrier showed up with a packet I had to sign for, paperwork for the separation agreement. It was the first time I'd talked to him since the accident. He scanned the bar code and tucked an electronic tablet back into his satchel. Then he cleared his throat.

"When the medics got there?" he said. "When you were telling them the kid had had a pulse? I should have spoken up, told them you were right."

"I should have let them do their job."

He thumbed the bill of his cap. "Truth is, at that point, I thought I might have imagined it."

"Didn't matter by then. If he was dead, he was dead."

"That was a bad feeling, not being able to *do* something." He told me he'd gone out and signed up for a CPR course the very next day. "Next time, I'm going to be ready."

Liz and I hadn't been apartment hunting since grad school, when she was at Weatherhead getting her MBA and I was at Cleveland State and it was just the two of us. Back then, we'd taken it as seriously as buying a house, inspecting every closet, every light fixture, every scratch on every hardwood floor. This time, we just wanted to get it over with. There would be no imagining ourselves studying together or throwing potlucks or sleeping in on weekends in these new places.

We got an early start on Saturday. We looked at an apartment building near the university that catered to students; a newer, more expensive one near the train station; and a loft over a nail salon downtown. Sara hated them all. When she wasn't crying, she was asking why we couldn't clean out the attic so I could have an apartment there.

On Sunday afternoon, we saw a furnished fourth-floor studio in a building that backed up to the railroad tracks. Sara stopped sulking long enough to watch a commuter train leave the station. The place was nothing special, but the fridge didn't smell, and there was no ring in the tub. I told the building manager I'd take it, and he went to get the contract. Waiting for him, I tried to picture myself eating at the little dinette, telling Sara good night over the phone, sleeping alone on the sofa bed. Liz had to step out into the hallway to pull herself together. Whereas I figured we'd be apart for a few weeks, max, she was presumably bracing herself for the whole two years. Not that I had much sympathy.

When the manager got back, I told him I wanted to go month to month. Liz took me aside and pointed out that a longer lease would be more convincing to a judge. I said I was planning to find a better place when we weren't in such a rush. She was too wrung out to argue. I signed a check for the deposit and first month's rent, the last one I'd write from our joint account.

Things moved quickly after that. On Monday, we finished the paperwork for the separation agreement and sent it back to Braun, at which point my name was on its way to being off of anything that mattered. On Tuesday, I called the cable company about internet service, stopped by the post office to change my address, and finished packing. On Wednesday, while Sara was at school, Helen arrived from Philadelphia in her Volvo with two suitcases and a frozen meat loaf.

"An apartment-warming gift," she said, handing it over. Then she stared at the file boxes stacked in the mudroom. "You're really going through with this?"

"Between you and me, I don't think it'll last."

I loaded the car before I went to pick up Sara so we could go straight to the apartment after I finished my crossing-guard shift. She had told her friends I was moving—"for a while," she was always careful to add—and by then most of the parents must have known, too. I was embarrassed to think they'd heard the ridiculous excuse Liz and I had given Sara, but we couldn't bring ourselves to tell her our marriage was in trouble. I told Liz that would be an even worse lie.

A few of the parents paused long enough in the cross-walk to say they were sorry to hear about Liz and me, or they hoped things worked out. It was awkward. Sara was about to become the only kid in her class whose parents weren't together. I wanted to tell them what I'd told Helen, that it wouldn't last, but they probably would have thought I was in denial, so I just said thanks. There wasn't time for much else. The fact that I was busy doing my job made things easier for everyone.

The apartment building's elevator was out of order, so Sara glumly held the emergency exit open as I carried in boxes from the car, her voice echoing after me in the stairwell— "Do you really have to do this, Dad?"—every plea a pinprick in my heart. Then we went back to the house for more. My suitcase was still open on the bed, half packed. Chairman Meow was curled up inside.

"Looks like you've got a stowaway," Helen said.

Sara lay down next to the suitcase. "He doesn't want you to go. Or he wants to come with you. So you don't get lonely."

I said I didn't plan on getting lonely since I'd be seeing her every day. But she was suddenly fixated on having the Chairman become my roommate, so I packed up the cat food and litter box and put him into his carrier. He wasn't mine to take—Liz and I had found him together, under the porch of our duplex in Cleveland Heights—but I could always bring him back if she wanted.

Sara and I spent the rest of the afternoon at the apartment. The Chairman stayed in the carrier for a while before he worked up the nerve to explore, keeping low and close to the walls. I unpacked my clothes. Sara went through a bin of toys and games she was planning to keep there. We built a fort out of empty moving boxes. She heard a train coming and decided we were runaways. The people on the train were trying to put us in an orphanage, she said. We hid in the fort, then unfolded the sofa bed to make a bigger fort underneath. She said the runaways were starving and sent me out to find food. When I came back with a box of crackers, which was all I had, she said, "Are you and mom taking a time-out?"

"Where'd you hear that?"

She said Lacy had said that sometimes when moms and dads weren't getting along, they decided to take a break.

"We're not taking a break," I said. "I just need a place to work."

"Well, when are you coming home?" she said, trying not to cry.

The trying was what really got me. "Soon," I said, hating myself for it. But Liz and I had agreed this would be our answer for as long as we could get away with it. She didn't want to tell Sara it would be two years, and I couldn't go behind her back and tell Sara otherwise.

"A week?" she said.

"Probably longer."

"A month?"

"It's hard to say."

She was holding a marker from her toy bin. She stabbed the back of my hand, hard, and crawled out of the fort. I went over to the window where she was standing and put my arms around her. Beyond the railroad tracks, next to a ball field, an ambulance was trying to get through traffic, but none of the cars were pulling over. The ambulance's siren echoed back and forth across the field until it sounded like there were five or six of them. Sara looked at the red dot on my hand.

" 'Soon' isn't a real answer," she said. " 'Soon' doesn't mean anything."

Liz had said I shouldn't meet her train anymore. She'd walk, or take the jitney, or drive herself. I'd said I had to bring Sara home anyway, so why wouldn't I be a decent future ex and pick her up?

On the ride home, she put on a brave face for Sara. She asked how the move went and nodded along, too enthusiastically, as Sara told her what a big help she'd been.

"But the window is painted shut," Sara said. "And the toilet doesn't flush all the way. I don't think Dad should move in until they fix everything."

I parked the station wagon in the garage, loaded a couple of boxes into my old hatchback, and came inside. Helen had a pot of chili going. I could feel Liz watching me as I got the sour cream out and started grating some cheddar. She put a hand on my arm.

"You should go."

"Braun said no spending the night. He didn't say anything about dinner."

"He said it has to be clear to the court that we intend to divorce."

"The court's not here," I said, and suggested a compromise: the minute there was a lawsuit, I wouldn't so much as set foot in the house.

In the end, she didn't seem to want to kick me out any more than I wanted to leave. I stayed for dinner and helped with the dishes, then the four of us played Parcheesi in front of a fire. It wasn't so different from any other time Helen had visited except that Sara kept looking at the clock and insisted on sitting on my lap for the whole game.

When it was bedtime, I tucked her in and said I'd see her in the morning.

"But you won't be here."

"Not when you wake up."

She started crying, abject sadness and need, asking me in between sobs to rub her back until she fell asleep. It took her almost an hour to settle down, but I was in no hurry. I sat there on the edge of the bed, trying to make out her face in the moonlight, thinking of all the times she'd called me in the night to take her to the bathroom or rescue a stuffed animal that had fallen on the floor.

It wasn't like we'd never spent a night apart, though. She'd spent weekends at Helen's; I'd traveled for work. This is nothing, I told myself.

But of course it didn't feel like nothing.

I was on my way out when Liz stopped me at the back door to ask how I was doing for money. She'd guessed how few hours I'd been billing since the accident.

"I can give you cash," she said, "but only under the table."

I told her no thanks, I was fine, and said I'd call in the morning, after I met with Tawana's attorney.

She shook her head. "You never called the lawyer I found, did you? You said you would."

"Our assets are being separated," I said. "Just like you wanted. If I get sued now, it's my business."

Helen cleared her throat. She was sitting on the patio with a cigarette and a glass of sherry. She said she didn't mean to eavesdrop, but she didn't see why we were so worried about getting sued. "It sounds like it was the guy's own fault."

"It was," I said, "which is why there won't be a lawsuit."

"Not that we can take the chance," Liz said.

"How long you do you want me to stay?" Helen said.

I told her the statute of limitations was two years.

Liz wasn't amused. "Just until I can find some help, Mom."

Helen lit another cigarette. She said she'd stay as long as we needed her.

Five minutes later, I was parked in front of the apartment building, staring at the red dot on the back of my hand. It was almost ten o'clock. Ten and a half hours to go before I picked Sara up for school. There was still unpacking to do, and I was falling further behind in my work, but I couldn't stand the idea of being alone in the apartment.

I wouldn't have minded a beer and some company, but most of my friends were back in Ohio and Kentucky. The people I knew in New Jersey were clients, neighbors, parents of kids in Sara's class—no one I could really talk to. I thought about calling my parents to tell them what was going on, then decided to wait, hoping I'd be back home before they ever found out.

I started the car again, thinking I might get some groceries, but eventually I found myself pulling up across the street from Derek's Custom Auto Body. I was surprised to see lights on at that hour. The Suburban guy was in the showroom, restocking shelves from open boxes on the floor. The sign on the door read CLOSED. I realized the place must be his—only an owner works that late. The idea of him passing for a respectable citizen disgusted me.

After a while, he put away the boxes, locked up, and drew a metal grate down over the window. The Suburban's headlights swept across my windshield as he was pulling out, and it occurred to me that he wouldn't recognize my car because I was driving the hatchback now.

I gave him half a block and tried to keep that distance between us as I tailed him past the bus depot, past the cemetery, and up into Montclair, but at some point he realized he was being followed. Maybe he was on guard, headed to a night deposit box with the day's receipts, or maybe I'd just been too obvious. He pulled over and waited for me to pass, then fell in behind me, his high beams filling the car's interior with light. My heart was going hard. I turned onto a side street and watched with a sinking feeling as he did the same, but I continued to drive as if nothing were going on, taking it easy, and eventually he gave up.

By the time he passed Sara's school, I was waiting for him.

* * *

He lived one street over from the school in a narrow two-story house with vinyl siding that had started to come loose under the eaves. He parked in the driveway and stopped for the mail on his way in. The porch, listing to one side, had two plastic chairs but no toys or bikes, nothing to suggest kids.

The lights came on downstairs, then upstairs. *What the hell am I doing here?* I thought. The answer was, nothing. It's not like I was going to *do* anything. But there was a satisfaction in watching him, as if I were gathering information that would be valuable to me in ways I didn't yet understand.

He was in the house for only a few minutes. When he came back out, he'd changed from his jeans and T-shirt into a track suit, just like he'd been wearing when I first saw him. This one was Adidas, unzipped at the neck to show off a gold chain. He peeled the magnetic sign off the door of the Suburban and tossed it inside.

I was more careful this time as I followed him to a nightclub on Bloomfield. There was a sandwich board on the sidewalk advertising a comedy open mic night. I gave him five minutes, then paid the cover, stood back by the bar, and ordered a beer. He was sitting with a baby-faced woman at a table up front. She had her hand on his neck and kept leaning her head against his when she spoke. They looked happy.

The show had already started, emceed by a deejay from a radio station I'd never heard of. Each comic got five minutes on the small stage, but I was so intent on the Suburban guy that I hardly noticed them. At some point the bartender told me there was a two-drink minimum. I ordered another beer. When I turned back around, the Suburban guy was making his way toward the stage. It hadn't occurred to me that he might be one of the comics, but it should have—who else goes to an open mic night? Seeing him up there smiling and waiting for the applause to die down, all I could think was, what an asshole.

I wanted him to flop. Someone would heckle him, he'd lose his temper, the police would come. But he'd done this before, you could tell. After introducing himself—he was Derek Dye, owner of a custom body shop—he started in with some jokes about having a storeroom full of spinning wheel covers nobody wanted anymore.

"Remember these?" He had one with him. He got it spinning and pretended to hypnotize somebody at a table up front. "You are getting very sleepy," he said. "Your Escalade needs a shiny new set of chrome spinners."

People were laughing. They kept laughing until his five minutes were up, and then they applauded and high-fived him as he came off the stage. If he had hiked his jacket and shown them his pistol, they probably would have laughed at that too. It was eleven-thirty, about the time Liz and I normally would have checked in on Sara before we went to bed. Derek and his girlfriend were heading toward the bar. Somebody clapped him on the back. Somebody else handed him a beer. I slipped out the door.

*　　*　　*

Liz called at five the next morning. She said she'd been up half the night worrying about my meeting. "Just call and say you can't do it until you get a lawyer."

I told her again that I thought showing up with a lawyer would only make it look like I had something to hide.

"Hello?" she said. "You do."

The Chairman was on the kitchen counter when I hung up, sniffing Helen's meat loaf, which I'd left out to thaw. I unwrapped the foil, put a little in his bowl with some cat food, and heated a slice for myself. Then I took a shower and tried to get some work done, but I was counting down the minutes until I saw Sara.

I ended up leaving early and had to kill time driving around the neighborhood. It was the coldest morning so far that fall. I came to a school bus with its sign out and stopped, but the two cars behind me went right on around. The bus driver then angled the bus so that he was blocking the street. Three kids got on. Two boys in the back, not much older than Sara, stared me down.

Helen had a cup of coffee waiting at the house. Liz gave me the lawyer's number again and offered to call Braun for more references. Sara came running down the stairs with a mouthful of toothpaste, greeting me as if I'd been gone for months before remembering to pretend she didn't care.

"Miss me?" she said in an accusing tone.

But we patched things up on the way to school, making plans to build a more elaborate fort, and we were still doing okay right up until I noticed the calendar on her classroom door. I was scheduled to be the parent helper that morning. It had completely slipped my mind. I was apologizing to Sara's teacher, telling her I'd have to come after my appointment, when Sara realized what was going on.

"You're supposed to be here this morning," she said.

"I will be," I said. "Just later."

"You're supposed to be here *now*."

Not ten minutes after I left, as I was merging onto the parkway, the school nurse called to say Sara wasn't feeling well. I had her put Sara on. She said her stomach hurt.

"Why didn't you say something before?"

"It didn't hurt before."

Liz was already on her way to work, so I suggested Sara have the nurse call Helen to come get her, but she began crying and said no, she wanted *me*. I turned around at the next exit.

I called home to let Helen know I was bringing Sara back, but she didn't answer the phone, and Sara started begging to go with me, promising she'd be good. I figured it couldn't hurt for Tawana's lawyer to meet her. Knowing his client's son almost killed a little girl and actually seeing her face-to-face were two different things. Perhaps he had kids of his own.

The practice was located in East Orange, in a big Victorian that had been converted into offices. On the way in, hurrying through the November chill, I started to ask Sara not to talk about the accident while we were there, then reconsidered; I didn't want her telling anyone she wasn't allowed to. We were ten minutes late, but it didn't matter. The lawyer, Raymond Burris, was running behind schedule. When he came out of his office in a pinstriped suit, Sara was assuring me she wasn't too sick for the class play that night. She fell silent and slid closer to me, and then I saw why: he was with Tawana Richards. I was tempted to get up and leave. Nobody had said anything about her being there. I felt like I'd walked into a trap.

But Tawana seemed as surprised as I was. After an awkward moment, she put out her hand and introduced herself, saying she hadn't properly done so before. She looked nothing like the last time I'd seen her. Her eyes were clear, her hair was pulled back, and she wore an expensive-looking dress and boots. She thanked me for coming.

"I didn't want Ray bothering you," she said, "but seeing as you're the only one who saw what happened—"

I said it was no trouble. Behind his smile, Burris looked uncomfortable. I'm sure he didn't want his client talking with a potential defendant.

"Hey there, young lady," he said to Sara. "No school today?"

"I'm sick."

"Sick?" He turned to his receptionist. "Monica, did you hear that? We've got a sick little girl over here." He touched Tawana's elbow. "If you'll excuse us, please, Mr. Bauer."

Burris helped Tawana with her jacket and led her to the door as the receptionist brought over a 7-Up and saltines for Sara. When he came back, he said if Sara was feeling up to it, he'd like for her to join us. I gave him the party line: she hadn't seen anything, she was going to a therapist, she'd been through a lot. He seemed disappointed, but he said he understood and ushered me into a room with bay windows and a marble fireplace. We sat at a coffee table instead of at his desk. He started by saying Tawana had told him how I'd taken her into my home. He said he imagined the accident had been quite an ordeal for me and my family. As he was talking, I noticed what looked like a framed photo of Juwan on the table. Maybe he saw me staring at it, or maybe it was part of his plan all along.

"That's him," he said, picking it up. "My sister's boy. I still can't believe it."

The family resemblance was suddenly clear. It was unnerving, like I was talking to an older, heavier version of Juwan himself. Burris held out the photo. I didn't want a closer look, but there was no avoiding it. Juwan was leaning against the Jaguar, clowning, his hands arranged in a criss-cross of signs. He looked like a kid who didn't take himself too seriously.

Burris went on to say he'd sponsored Juwan's baseball

teams for years. The team photos were in a row on the wall above a bookcase lined with trophies. He said Juwan had had a good arm for a skinny kid, and he'd been disappointed when he didn't go out for varsity. "But by then, it was all skateboarding."

With every word he spoke, I imagined him gauging my reaction. Surely he could tell how uneasy I was. The more he said, the worse I felt. Up to a point—when I'd listened to Liz read the obituary, or to Juwan's friends' stories at the funeral—I'd felt like I was taking my medicine, fulfilling some obligation. Now I'd had enough. Maybe Liz had been right. My lawyer, if I'd had one, would have put a stop to this.

But when Burris started pointing out Juwan in the photos, I couldn't very well just sit there. We stood together in front of the bookcase. Juwan was easy to spot. As a kid, he'd had his mom's hair, puffing out like hi-fi earphones from beneath his cap. Also the biggest, most disarming smile of any kid on the team, year after year.

Finally Burris took a seat and got down to business. He assured me he wasn't on a witch hunt. "Right now, I'm just trying to find out what happened."

He asked if I could start by telling him everything I remembered about the accident. I'd thought I wouldn't be nervous, as many times as I'd been over it, but surrounded by all those photos of Juwan, it was hard to concentrate. I managed to tell him what I'd told the police. He took notes. When I was done, he asked me to draw a diagram of the accident. He had questions, too: Did the town do a good job of maintaining our street? Were there any pot-holes or other chronic road conditions? How quickly did the police and medics arrive? What was my impression of the job they did?

Through it all, he addressed me as if I were on his side, a potential witness for the plaintiff. At no point did he give any indication that I was the only obvious defendant, and at no point did I acknowledge my awareness of this fact. I supposed he could have gone after the girlfriend's parents, if that's where the alcohol had come from, or the car dealer, if there turned out to have been some mechanical issue, or maybe the town itself, but those would have been long shots. I figured if he didn't have a case against me, he didn't have a case at all.

When we came out of his office, Sara was on her fifth pack of saltines. Burris asked how she was feeling, and she said, "Better." I didn't want them getting into a conversa-tion, so I got us out of there as quickly as I could.

Outside, I took Sara's hand, relieved. Liz would be wait-ing to hear how things went. No surprises, I'd tell her. No reason to think they'd actually sue. I was considering calling her right there in the parking lot, when I looked up and saw Tawana. She was waiting at our car in a long suede jacket with a fur collar, her arms folded against the cold.

"Mr. Bauer?" she said, squaring her shoulders. "I won't keep you. I just wanted to say I'm sorry for the other day. For imposing on you. Sara, I'm sorry if I frightened you."

I remembered the look on Sara's face after Tawana had taken the axe to the tree. Now she was practically hiding behind me.

"That's okay," she said.

"I want you to know that's not who I am, Mr. Bauer," Tawana said. "And I'm not the kind of person who goes around suing people, either. My brother, he's just doing what he has to." She glanced at Burris's window, where he stood watching us. "I realize that crash was my son's fault. I don't like it, but I accept it. This business where something bad happens, somebody automatically gets sued—" She shook her head, holding back tears. "That's not going to bring my boy back."

I just stood there, at a loss. The idea of Tawana apologizing to me was almost too much. I wanted to cover my ears. At the same time, hearing her say the accident had been Juwan's fault almost felt like she was *forgiving* me, though I knew how absurd that was. She didn't know what I'd done and surely wouldn't have forgiven me if she had. At any moment, I was certain she'd look into my eyes and see me for what I was.

"Anyhow," she said, "don't take this wrong, but I hope this is the last time we meet. It's just too hard."

I managed to nod and say I understood as I opened the door for Sara to get in. Tawana turned to her, blinking, as if she'd forgotten she were there. Then her expression softened, and she put a hand to Sara's cheek.

"Poor baby," she said. "You must have been so scared."

I knew how uncomfortable Sara was, but I remember hoping she'd at least be polite. And in fact I think that's exactly what she was aiming for. I'm sure she didn't mean for what she said to come out sounding like a boast.

"Not really," she said. "Not like the first time."

Looking back, I suppose it must seem like I *wanted* to get caught. Why else would I have been standing outside Burris's office, letting Sara talk to Tawana? Why else would I have brought her along in the first place when I could have just taken her back to the apartment and rescheduled the meeting?

Now it was out of my hands. There was nothing to do but hope Tawana didn't understand what Sara was saying, that she'd just let it go. But she was too nice for that.

"First time, baby?" She gave Sara a blank sort of smile. "First time what?"

"That he almost hit us," Sara said. "We stopped so fast, the seat belt hurt my shoulder."

I was already buckling her in, silently begging her to be quiet.

"Who?" Tawana said. "Juwan?"

Sara nodded. Tawana looked to me for help. I turned up my palms.

"You mean that guy on Thomas Boulevard?" I said. "The one who stopped in the middle of the street?"

"No, Daddy. I spilled my grapes, remember?"

"That was the man in the SUV. I think you're getting them confused."

"No, I'm not."

"Juwan was in a convertible," I said, "not an SUV."

"I'm *talking* about the convertible." She made a face and slapped her knee. I must have seemed like some stranger who'd taken over her dad's body.

"It's okay, baby," Tawana said. "I'm just glad you weren't scared."

I realized Tawana was barely holding it together. All that talk about the accident must have taken a toll. That and possibly just seeing Sara, being in the presence of someone else's living, breathing child. I closed Sara's door and apologized for her.

"No need," Tawana said. "Juwan was the same way, so *stubborn* sometimes—" She caught herself and smiled, to show me she didn't mean any offense, but the tears were already coming. Sara crossed her arms and scowled at us. Burris was still at the window, probably wondering if he should come out and put a stop to whatever was going on. I felt like crawling under the car. As much as I wanted to get out of there, though, I couldn't just drive off and leave Tawana like that. I waited until she got control of herself. She blew her nose and took out her keys.

"He was a good boy," she said. "I know it must not seem like it, but it's true."

"I'm sure he was."

119

She looked at me like I still needed convincing. "He just made some bad decisions."

I nodded. "Like everybody does."

Once upon a time, I didn't think I wanted kids. In fact, even after you were born, there were days when I felt that becoming a parent was something I'd done for you and your mom, not for myself. I got over that in a hurry, but the shame of it has never completely gone away. There are still days I know I don't deserve you.

"Why did you say that?" Sara said. "Why did you make her not believe me?"

I was driving her back to school, hating myself for running roughshod over her, wishing there had been another way. And it was only going to get worse, because now she'd go tell her mom, looking for sympathy, and Liz would realize there was still more about the accident I'd kept to myself.

"I'm sorry, sweetie. Sometimes people remember things differently."

Our eyes met in the rearview mirror. She was staring at me in disbelief. She knew perfectly well what she'd seen. She knew perfectly well what *I'd* seen.

I pulled over and killed the engine. "You know what? Maybe you're right. Maybe I'm the one who got confused."

At first she wouldn't even come up front. Then, after she had a long cry, she gave me a solemn stare. "I accept your apology."

That was something she'd learned in school, instead of saying "That's all right" when really it wasn't. She wiped her eyes and leaned her head on my chest. I could have sat there like that all day, feeling the weight of her, listening to the traffic go by.

My phone beeped, a text message from Liz. All it said was, "So?"

Might as well get it over with, I thought. Sara was going to tell her what happened sooner or later. At least this way, I'd know what was said. I dialed Liz's office and told her Sara was with me, that she hadn't been feeling well so I'd brought her along to the lawyer's office. Then I put her on speaker, hoping for the best.

"Hi, butterfly," Liz said. "I'm sorry you don't feel good."

"I feel better," Sara said. "Dad and I were having a fight, but now we're making up."

"Oh, no. About what?"

"About the dead boy—"

"Not a fight," I said. "A disagreement. I remembered something wrong, and Sara corrected me."

Sara liked the sound of that. "I have the best memory in the family. That's what Nana says."

121

"Tawana was there," I said, changing the subject. "She was waiting for us after the meeting. She apologized for the accident and said it was his F-A-U-L-T."

"Why are you spelling?" Sara said. "What's the secret?"

"She said she wasn't the kind of person who goes around S-U-I-N-G."

"She really said that?" Liz said. "I mean, you have to admit, it's almost too perfect."

"What's 'suing,'" Sara said. "Will someone please let me into the conversation?"

"Hey." I took her nose between my knuckles. "How about some ice cream before we go back?"

When the three of us went out for burgers after the class play that night, nobody called it a celebration, but that's how it felt to me—just the fact that Liz was okay with our being seen in public. She'd had time to think over what Tawana had said. She still wasn't going to get her hopes up, but she wasn't going to ignore a little bit of light at the end of the tunnel, either. Now it was just a matter of waiting to make sure we were in the clear. Her main concern was Rizzo.

"Because if he presses charges," she said, while Sara was in the bathroom, "Tawana will change her mind. She'd almost have to."

That night, as I was tucking Sara in and telling her what a good, authentic Pilgrim she'd been, I remember thinking

I'd been right to go along with the separation after all, just as I'd been right in thinking it wouldn't last. Liz was starting to seem like a reasonable human being again. We had hurt Sara, but she'd get over it. I only wished there were some way to let her know that now, soon really did mean soon.

Telling Liz good-bye was even stranger now that there seemed so little point in our being separated. I was hoping she'd say enough was enough and ask me to stay the night. I was still hoping on the drive home, expecting it to be her when my phone rang.

"Rizzo here," the detective said.

I asked him to hold on and pulled over, wishing I hadn't answered, wishing I hadn't had a beer at dinner. "What can I do for you, Detective?"

He was curt. He said he'd appreciate my coming to his office the next morning. "More questions." There was a siren in the background, voices and traffic.

"Sure," I said. What else could I say? I closed the phone and sat there, whipsawed, trying to imagine what could be so important that he'd call at ten-fifteen, from what sounded like the scene of a crash. Whatever it was, he'd been all business. I felt like a fool for having believed, even briefly, that the accident was behind us. It was like Liz had said: did I really think there weren't going to be consequences? And now I surely had it coming—lying to Tawana's face the way I had, twisting Sara's words.

The OUT OF ORDER sign was gone from the elevator. My phone rang again as I was waiting. This time it really was Liz, calling to say Rizzo was trying to reach me.

"I gave him your number," she said. "I told him you'd moved out."

"He just called. He wants me to come downtown for more questions."

"Oh, God, not again."

There wasn't much else to say. I pushed the elevator button a second time. Either someone was holding it, or it was still broken.

Lying in bed that night with Chairman Meow at my feet, I wanted to believe Rizzo was just trying to scare me. But what if he wanted me to take a lie detector test? What if he'd come up with proof I'd lied about the photos? What if he'd found another witness? It would be my word against theirs, and mine wasn't much more than a balloon waiting to be popped.

By the time I dropped Sara off at school, I was imagining myself not coming home. I hugged her for so long, she asked what was wrong.

"Let's do something special this afternoon," I said. "Anything you want."

*   *   *

The prosecutor's office was in the county courthouse. I parked in the garage and went in the back, joining the line of people waiting to go through security. Just being inside the building, surrounded by so many police officers and lawyers, made me feel like I didn't have a chance. After the metal detector, I took an escalator up to the main floor and found the elevators. Six or seven jurors were waiting to go up to one of the courtrooms; I was the only person who got off on the fifth floor.

I told the woman behind the thick glass I was there to see Rizzo. He came out a few minutes later. Still all business. I followed him to an anonymous-looking office. Behind a metal desk, a small window gave onto a sliver of downtown Newark. A few personal items were lined up on the sill like pieces of evidence that he actually worked there: a chipped coffee mug with "Dad" on it, a cactus, a Rubik's Cube that had either been solved or never touched.

After he closed the door, Rizzo said he was sorry to hear Liz and I were having trouble. "Been there. Not fun." Then he asked how Sara was.

I said she was fine, that we still saw each other every day.

"Good for you," he said, motioning for me to sit. He took down my new address on an old-fashioned Rolodex card, then laced his fingers on the desk. "Here's the situation. I was speaking with Tawana Richards yesterday, and she mentioned running into you and Sara. She said Sara claimed you were involved in a separate incident with Juwan prior to the accident."

He leaned back in his chair, waiting for me to take it from there. I just stared. I didn't believe Tawana thought what Sara had said was worth reporting. Maybe she happened to mention it to Burris and he'd encouraged her to call, or maybe Rizzo had spoken with her for some other reason and it had just come up.

"Is that correct, Mr. Bauer?"

"Yes, that's what she said." The words were like glue in my mouth. "But it was a misunderstanding. She got him confused with a different guy we saw on the drive home that day."

"Ms. Richards indicated she was quite insistent."

"She's six," I said. "She doesn't like being told she's wrong."

"She's an eyewitness to a fatal car accident." Rizzo came around and sat on the corner of the desk, close enough that I could smell the wool of his suit. "Look, Sara could clear this up. I've interviewed kids before. If you're worried about me upsetting her—"

"It's not that. I just think—my wife and I both—she's been through enough. Like we said."

"Let me ask you something, Mr. Bauer. Do you ever think about what *his* family's been through?"

Rizzo was finally showing his true colors. Outside, sunlight glinted off a high-rise, but the window was so narrow, I couldn't tell which direction I was looking in.

"It's been three weeks," I said, trying to remain civil. "If she knew anything, it would have come out by now."

When I didn't—couldn't—meet his eye, he went back to his chair. He knew I was lying; that much was clear. What I needed to know was whether he'd figured out why. That would give him a motive, which for all I knew was the only thing stopping him from pressing charges.

"You're putting me in a tough spot here," he said. "Without Sara, all I've got to go on is a report that the only person besides you who saw the accident made a statement that contradicts what you've told me."

When I still didn't have anything to say for myself, he proceeded to tell me I had the right to remain silent, that anything I said could and would be held against me in a court of law, that I had the right to an attorney, and that if I couldn't afford one, one would be appointed to me. Then he asked if I understood.

What I understood was this: now that he knew I knew he thought I was lying, he could stop pretending I was just a witness. I was officially a suspect. I didn't have to tiptoe anymore, either. I ignored the blood pounding in my temples.

"Are you arresting me?"

"No."

"Are you taking me into custody?"

"I'd say you're in a custodial situation. Do you understand your rights or not?"

"I do," I said. "I don't need a lawyer."

"So you're willing to continue?"

He seemed mildly surprised. I guess I was, too. I was ready for whatever he had, one way or another. Wasting no time, he took out his pen and asked what my route had been on the day of the accident. After I'd laid it out for him, street by street, he gave a nod, as if I'd confirmed what he already knew. Then he opened a file folder on his desk and took out a sheet of paper. He said he was holding a statement he'd gotten yesterday from a village patrolman who'd seen a silver Jaguar convertible pass through a safety checkpoint just prior to the accident.

"He remembered the vehicle because it exited the checkpoint at a high rate of speed. He said it made a sharp turn onto Kingsley, into your neighborhood. That puts you and Juwan in the same place at about the same time."

"I remember the checkpoint."

"And the convertible?"

I shook my head.

"Mr. Bauer, are you aware of the penalties for making a false statement?"

"I think so." I wasn't, but I didn't want to hear them. I was waiting for the other shoe to drop, for him to tell me what else the officer had seen. Instead, he sat back and waited too. We must have sat like that, silent, for one or two minutes, though it felt much longer. At some point, it occurred to me he might be bluffing. Because what did he really have? Even if he was able to prove I'd lied about seeing Juwan twice, that didn't prove I'd caused the accident, much less that I'd cut the wheel on purpose. Maybe he didn't have anything else, so all he could do was try to trick me into talking.

"Why didn't they stop him at the checkpoint?" I said.

"Why should they? Because he was a black kid in a Jaguar?"

"Because he was drunk."

"You're from down South," he said. "Kentucky. Isn't that right?"

It took me a moment to see what he was getting at. "This is bullshit."

He leaned forward, smiling a little, looking pleased to have gotten a rise out of me. "Here's what comes next," he said. "I start knocking on doors until I find somebody who saw what happened after he made that turn. If you have anything to tell me, I suggest you do it before then."

"Am I free to go?"

He came around from his desk and opened the door. "Yes, you are."

I left the courthouse shaking all over, feeling like I might be sick, but Rizzo still wasn't finished. Halfway back to the apartment, I got a call from Liz. He'd reached her at work, asking her for permission to speak with Sara.

"Unbelievable," I said. "I just told him no, not ten minutes ago."

She said maybe it was different now that we were separated; maybe he needed permission from only one of us. "What if he shows up at her school?"

"He can't do that," I said.

"He can do whatever he wants."

"I'm going to get Sara. We'll come into the city." I needed to tell Liz how things had gone with Rizzo, but not over the phone, not with fifteen miles and a river between us.

"That's all right," she said. "You don't have to do that." But she sounded relieved.

I drove straight to school, told Warren I couldn't do the crosswalk, and signed Sara out. Even though I knew Rizzo wasn't going to show up, it made me feel better having her with me. I told her I was taking her to Central Park.

"That's the something special?" she said. "I thought I got to pick."

On the train, Sara sat on my lap for a better view, and as the houses and apartment buildings flashed by, it was all I could do not to lock my arms around her. The fact that I wasn't going to be moving back home anytime soon was bad enough, but what if I really did get arrested? How would I explain that to her? I pictured Rizzo, already in our neighborhood, chatting up lawn crews, meter readers, jitney drivers, residents—anyone who might have been around to see us on Kingsley that day. There were ten or twelve houses on that block. All it would take was one person who'd happened to glance out the window when they heard the Jaguar come racing in off South Orange Avenue.

If only I hadn't brought Sara along to that meeting. If only I hadn't stood there like an idiot letting her talk to Tawana.

Sara was too excited about our trip to notice what a basket case I was. "Do I still get to do anything I want?" She couldn't decide between the carousel and the playground with the big granite slide.

"We'll do both," I said.

Outside, factories and warehouses gave way to wetlands crisscrossed by truss bridges and raised highways. Along the rail bed, old power lines drooped from tilted poles into water dotted with discarded tires. The scenery wasn't enough to hold Sara's attention. She slid off my lap and took a notebook from her backpack. I called Helen to tell her we were going into the city. When I hung up, Sara was drawing a tree with branches that looked like arms.

"Is that Sicky?"

She snapped the notebook shut and shook her head. After the way things had gone with Tawana, I could hardly blame her for being guarded. I turned back to the window, not wanting to make her any more self-conscious than I already had, but we were entering the tunnel, and there was nothing to look at on either side of us now but darkness.

*   *   *

Liz got away from work and met us at the playground, and the three of us walked over to the carousel. Sara was careful choosing a horse. Liz and I stood back so we could hear ourselves over the calliope. As the ride started, Sara let out a whoop and waved to us—pure, carefree happiness. I didn't want to be the one who took that away from her.

"He read me my rights," I said.

Liz stopped waving. She looked stricken. She put her arms around my neck and pressed her head into my chest. Sara went past on the carousel three times, staring at us, before Liz pulled herself together.

"So what happened?" she said. "You stopped talking and then what? Tell me you didn't keep talking."

When I didn't answer, her arms fell away. She straightened up and wiped her cheeks. She took a step back, squinting at me as if I were a blur.

"What is wrong with you, Glen? Are you *trying* to get caught?"

I started to tell her what I'd been telling myself, that Rizzo would have arrested me if he could, but she turned away, disgusted. By now the ride was over and Sara was coming through one of the carousel's brick archways, asking for a hot pretzel. She stopped short when she got a look at us. "What's wrong?"

We each forced a smile, said "nothing" at the same time. Sara frowned. She took Liz's hand and mine and pressed them together.

"Come on," she said. "Make up."

*   *   *

Liz took Sara back to her office that afternoon and gave two weeks' notice. She didn't tell me until that night, on the phone. Now that I was a suspect, she said, a lawsuit was almost guaranteed. We had to get serious about the separation, keep up appearances. For all we knew, I might even be under surveillance at some point. No more staying for dinner, no more putting Sara to bed.

"Under surveillance?" I said.

Liz skipped right over that. If she was ever going to stay home with Sara, she said, now was the time. "Things are only going to get harder for her." She said she'd be working for herself, as a consultant, like we'd talked about. She had savings. She was good for six months. If it didn't work out, she said, she could always get another job—and I believed it. She apparently had a gift for recruiting. She'd been recruited by other banks herself. What I didn't believe was that she hadn't bothered talking any of this over with me first.

"What the hell, Liz? Do I not even exist?"

"Like you said, if you get sued now, that's your business. This is mine."

For the first time, I had to agree with her about the likelihood of a lawsuit. We sat Sara down in the kitchen the next day to explain why things were going to be different. We told her we had decided to take a break after all. We weren't getting a divorce, but we had some issues to work out. I'd thought it would be easier with her than before—partly because we'd already taken the first, worst step, and partly because this time it wasn't a perverse, unnecessary lie—we really *did* have things to work out.

"Grown-up stuff," Liz said. "It has nothing to do with you, butterfly."

"How long of a break?"

Liz and I looked at each other.

"I knew it," Sara said. "I knew it wasn't about work."

She pushed away from the table and ran upstairs. By the time we caught up with her, she'd already tipped her book-shelf over and was pulling drawers out of her dresser, calling us liars. Neither of us tried to stop her. We just sat on the bed, hoping she'd come to us when she was done.

We worked out a new schedule, which Liz had Braun put into the separation agreement. She took Sara to school; I picked her up. I had her every other weekend and until seven on weeknights. Each afternoon, as soon as I was finished with the crosswalk, I'd take her to a park, a play-ground, a movie. Having something to do or somewhere to be seemed important. A couple of times she brought along a friend. Once we went roller-skating. If the weather was bad, we came back to the apartment and played Monopoly while Chairman Meow tried to lie on the board. Sara was generally a good sport. She went along. No matter what we did, though, sadness hung from her like a heavy coat. She slumped; she shuffled. Now and then—on a tire swing at the park, or collecting Boardwalk rent from me—she'd light up like she used to, smiling and laughing, but only for a moment.

I'd keep her right up until the buzzer, 6:55, then drive her home and tell her good night on the front steps. Liz would meet us at the door, and we'd visit for a few minutes, both of us pretending, for Sara's sake and ours, that we were all doing okay.

I went ahead and called Linda Schwartz, the lawyer Liz's coworker had recommended. Now that Rizzo openly distrusted me, there was no point worrying how it would look. I told her I was a suspect in the police investigation of a fatal car crash. She agreed to meet with me. The next day, I drove to an office building in Jersey City and sat in the parking deck, staring at my hands on the wheel, remembering how I'd cut it back and forth. I stared long enough that they began to seem separate from my body, like someone else's hands.

During our meeting, I told Schwartz the same half-truths I'd told Burris and the police; I told her about my conversations with Rizzo; I told her there had been a misunderstanding with Sara that had led the detective to consider me a suspect. I figured that was all she needed to know. The important thing was, I was getting a lawyer.

I was looking forward to telling Liz, but Schwartz's assessment was only half encouraging. If the autopsy report showed Juwan really had been drinking, she said, a grand jury might feel he'd gotten what he deserved. In her opinion, the case would probably never go to trial, if they even got so far as charging me, which she doubted they would since their evidence was purely circumstantial.

"But the civil suit," she said. "That could still be huge."

The time I spent with Sara felt like actual living. The rest just felt like waiting, to see her again or for something to give—for the investigation to be over, one way or another. Part of the problem was the autopsy report. I figured once there was proof Juwan had been drinking, Rizzo would have to close the case. If nothing else, the prosecutor would make him move on. But the report wasn't due back until January at the earliest. Three to six months, he'd said. The lag time boggled my mind. Wasn't it cruel to make Juwan's family wait so long? And what about me? How was I even going to know when it was done? It wasn't as if Rizzo would go out of his way to tell me.

I got so impatient, I ended up calling the medical examiner's office myself, not caring if Rizzo found out. For all I knew, they'd finished the report early. The clerk said she couldn't tell me anything, though. I told her I knew the reports were a matter of public record.

"Not if they're part of an ongoing case," she said.

All I could do was try to stay busy, but at that time of the year, I typically had more time than work to fill it. I did what I could, meeting with clients, updating software, studying changes in the tax code. An accounting firm in Newark was looking to farm out some bookkeeping, and despite the so-so pay, I took it on. I even put out feelers on the job market, though I wasn't ready to do anything that would jeopardize my time with Sara.

Thanksgiving came and went. For the first time since college, I didn't spend the day with Liz. I took Sara out for lunch, and she had a real dinner with her mom and Helen that night. I ended up downtown at The Gaslight, drank a couple of pints, then went for a long walk, until I was tired enough to sleep.

And that became my routine. I'd work late, swing by the pub, then head out, walking all over town—everywhere except Tawana's neighborhood. It wouldn't have surprised me if she'd been wandering the streets herself at that hour, and the prospect of seeing her terrified me. By then she must have known I was a suspect. Rizzo would have told her.

Probably he'd done it the minute I left his office, eager to see her put the legal screws to me, even if he couldn't manage to bring criminal charges himself. Now that a lawsuit couldn't hurt Liz and Sara, though, the money hardly mattered to me; I just didn't want to face Tawana again. If she sued, I intended to settle right away. I'd let Schwartz handle it all. They could take a cut of my earnings for the rest of my life. Whatever else of mine Tawana wanted, she could have—not that there was much left.

But as November turned to December with no word from Burris, I could only conclude that Tawana had meant what she'd said about not suing. That, or they didn't have enough of a case until I was actually charged with a crime—which, despite Rizzo's threats, seemed less likely with each passing day.

Sometimes I'd leave the pub at eleven and not get home until after one. But no matter what direction I started off in, inevitably I'd end up on the east end of town, in front of our house, looking up at Sara's window. One night a couple of weeks before Christmas, out of curiosity, I walked up the drive to see if Liz's car was there. She was home and still awake; she noticed the security light come on. As I was looking through the garage window, she opened the back door.

"Glen? Is that you?"

She came out onto the patio wearing an old pea coat of mine over her flannel pajamas. I thought she'd ask me to leave, but instead she offered me a sip of her wine. She said she'd seen me out in front of the house twice. I asked how she was holding up.

"Could we not talk about us?" she said, turning up her collar.

"Okay. How's work?"

Before she even left the bank, they'd offered her a six-month contract—the same work she'd been doing, but on a consulting basis.

"Pay's not what it used to be," she said, "but I'm only going in three or four times a week, and only for a few hours. I can do the rest here."

"I'll help out," I said. "Once things pick up. We'll be fine."

Her silence was like a finger against my lips. I mentioned my bookkeeping gig. I said I'd have a check for her at the beginning of the month, every month. She said she didn't need it.

"Then you can put it in the bank. It'll be safer in your account than mine. Isn't that the idea?"

She said fine, she'd have Braun add something about child support to the agreement.

"Speaking of lawyers," I said, "I met with Linda Schwartz." I hadn't mentioned it sooner because I didn't want to go into what she'd said about a civil suit. But now I told Liz I'd agreed not to speak with the police or Burris again without Schwartz there.

"I wish you hadn't waited so long. But it's good you went." Stamping her feet, she passed me the glass again and said I should finish it. Across the street, the memorial shone in the moonlight. A cross now stood among the flowers. Fresh bouquets had continued to arrive despite the frost.

"Sara ends up in bed with me most nights," she said. "She asks when you're coming home."

"Yesterday she accused me of not even wanting to."

Liz blew into her hands and reached for the empty glass. "You better go. It's freezing out here. And don't tell her you came by, okay? She'll stay up looking for you."

The next night, when I brought Sara home, I waited until she was inside, then told Liz it wasn't worth it anymore. I tried to be diplomatic. I said I could understand why things had had to change after Rizzo turned up the heat, but it had been a month now. Whatever he'd told Tawana hadn't changed her mind about not suing.

"What's a month?" Liz said. "They have two years."

"But look what we're doing to Sara. What's the point of protecting our assets if we're not protecting her?"

Glancing at the house, Liz admitted she sometimes felt the same way. She said every night that Sara cried herself to sleep, she did too. "But we'll regret it if we're short-sighted. We have to think about the rest of her life."

"*This* is her life," I said. "Now. And it's going to leave a mark."

She gave me a tired look. She said couples separated all the time, and of course it wasn't pretty but the kids turned out fine. "Besides, it's not like she doesn't see us both, it's not like we fight in front of her, it's not like it's even permanent. It's the most benign separation in the history of marriage."

"In any case," I said, "I'm coming home."

I went back to the apartment and repacked a few boxes. I knew Liz might flip out, but it also seemed like she might not. I at least had to try. The next morning, I was at the house, getting ready to unload the car, when she came home from taking Sara to school.

"Bring a single box inside," she said, "and I'll get a restraining order."

"If that's what you feel like you have to do." I carried a box past her and up to my office. By the time I got back downstairs, she was on the phone, calling Braun. I still thought she might not go through with it. I wished Helen were there to put in her two cents, but she'd gone back to Philadelphia for the week.

"Please," I said. "Hang up the phone."

Liz didn't blink. She was waiting for Braun to answer. She said she didn't want to kick me out in front of Sara, but I wasn't giving her much choice. "What are you going to do? Tell her you're home, then leave again when they hand you the papers?"

When Braun picked up, she turned her back on me, asking him what she needed to do. "No," she said. "He's here, but he's not violent or anything."

I came around and stood in front of her, hoping the sight of me would make a difference, but I might as well have been standing in front of a wall.

"All right. You can stop now. I'm going."

On the last day of school before Christmas break, after Liz and I finished divvying up Sara's wish list on the phone, she asked if I'd spoken with Schwartz about anything other than the accident. I think she was afraid I'd start fighting the separation.

"No," I said.

"Braun says I should go ahead with the restraining order. In case you try again."

"I'm not planning to."

"Good. I told him no anyway. I'd never do that—I mean, unless I really had to."

I took the opportunity to suggest that the three of us spend Christmas at my parents' in Kentucky, where no one would know we weren't supposed to be together. I even offered to take a separate flight, but Liz said no, arguing that at some point we might have to sign an affidavit attesting to the particulars of our separation. She said Sara could go to Covington with me after Christmas, just the two of us. I looked out at the snow coming down on the railroad tracks. When I'd finally gotten around to telling my parents what was going on, I tried to make them understand it was only temporary, but they didn't believe me. Showing up without Liz would only make things worse.

"No," I said. "I can't go without you." Then I suggested we all spend Christmas together anyway—even divorced couples get together on holidays for the sake of the kids, I pointed out—but Liz wouldn't budge. Too tired for another showdown, I eventually agreed to Sara's spending Christmas Eve with me and Christmas Day with her and Helen.

By the time I got to school, the snow was falling harder, straight down like rain. A storm had arrived sooner than expected, and the salt trucks weren't out yet. I got my gear and headed for the crosswalk. I'd already told Warren it would be my last day. The job was cutting into my time with Sara, and she didn't like having to wait around for me after school.

When her class let out, she came over to the fence and asked if she could go home with Lacy. I reminded her that we were going to Maplewood to pick out a Christmas tree for the apartment.

"It's your apartment," she said. "Why do I have to pick out the tree?"

A boy from her class, Ted, was waiting to cross the street, eating a bag of M&M's. His mother, Rachel, gave me a

sympathetic look. I hated being the first grade's token es-
tranged husband. I held up my sign and motioned for them
to cross, but halfway into the street, Ted spilled his candy,
red and green M&Ms dotting the snow. As he knelt to re-
trieve them, a pickup crested the hill and braked too late. It
fishtailed into the intersection. The driver laid on the horn.
Ted panicked and slipped in the snow. I grabbed him by
his jacket and shoved him toward the curb. Rachel caught
him as the pickup's fender collided with my shoulder. I went
sprawling in the snow and rolled, trying not to get run over,
but the truck must have already stopped.

Before I knew what was happening, Rachel and the
driver were helping me up, asking if I was okay. As far as I
could tell, I was fine. Ted was in tears, clinging to his mom.
Sara came running from the school yard. Traffic stopped in
all directions. The driver was practically in tears himself. He
kept apologizing, half in what sounded like Arabic—to me,
to Ted, to Rachel.

Somebody said the police were on the way. I didn't want
to talk to them but knew I'd have to. Warren took control of the crosswalk and started directing traffic around the
pickup. An ambulance arrived. The medics looked Ted over,
then me. Warren overheard me declining a ride to the hospital for a more thorough examination. He told me I should
go, even if I felt fine. He said I was full of adrenaline and
might not know if I was hurt.

"You could wake up tomorrow and not be able to get
out of bed."

A TV news van showed up while Sara and I were wait-ing for the police to finish with the driver. They'd been out doing weather stories, on their way to a pileup on Route 46, when they heard about our mishap on the police radio. The reporter, a young guy in a puffy jacket and leather gloves, came over with the cameraman and a microphone, but I told them I didn't want to be on TV. It was all too eerily familiar.

"I don't like this," Sara said. "I want to go home."

"We will. Soon as they let me leave."

Even though I hadn't done anything wrong, I was ner-vous explaining to the police what had happened. The news crew got some footage of me talking to them. Afterward, they asked again for an interview but had to settle for Ted, who seemed to be enjoying the attention, and Rachel, who claimed I'd saved her son's life.

Sara thought I was a hero. That's what she told the old men from the Rotary Club who sold us our Christmas tree, and that's what she told Liz and Helen on the front porch when I dropped her off.

"It was just luck," I said. "I was lucky to be standing right there."

"Not lucky," Sara said. "Brave."

"The truck actually hit you?" Helen said. "Are you sure you're okay?"

I windmilled my arm. "Just a little sore."

I was hoping Liz would take pity and ask me to stay for dinner. Instead, she said she was glad I was quitting.

"Me too," Sara said. "And I'm glad school's out."

We had plans to go sledding at Flood's Hill the next day while Liz was in the city. I looked over at the memorial, now covered in white except for the cross. "Let's hope it doesn't let up."

Driving back to the apartment, I was at loose ends. I didn't feel like working; I didn't feel like being alone. At The Gaslight, the bartender, Dan, was surprised to see me so early. I told him I was celebrating—I'd saved a kid from getting hit by a truck. He listened to the story, then poured me a pint on the house. When I was done, I tipped him double, and he poured another. Outside, a plow rumbled by, followed by a salt truck. A basketball game was on TV, interrupted now and then by a train whistle. I ordered a sandwich and fries. The stools around the U-shaped bar began to fill with commuters. I sat there sipping my beer, wanting to feel good about what I'd done. I wanted the news to come on TV and to hear Rachel say I'd saved Ted's life and have Dan and everybody else there hear it too. I wanted them to know that about me as badly as I'd wanted the people in that other bar to know about Derek Dye. I found myself considering the possibility that saving Ted in some way made up for what had happened with Juwan. Except that even after three beers, I knew that was horseshit. Lives weren't figures in a ledger, and what was done was done. There were just consequences, how you felt, and what you did about it.

On the way to Montclair, I picked up a cold six-pack and was already cracking the first one as I parked across the street from Derek's. I stashed the rest in the console, zipped my coat, and put the window down. Snowflakes drifted in. The upstairs lights were on in the house. After a few minutes, I caught a glimpse of Derek in boxers and an undershirt, getting dressed. I pictured his pistol on the dresser. I imagined how it would feel to turn the gun on him.

Ever since I'd followed him to the club, I'd had it in the back of my mind that I was going to do something about him. The problem was, I didn't know what. I'd been telling myself I had time, that the longer I waited, the sweeter it would be, but I knew this was just a way of letting myself off the hook. Believing I'd do something had become more important than actually doing it.

Now that I was sitting there in the dark, though, watching him, I felt obliged to consider a course of action. I wasn't going to shoot him or run him down, like I'd wanted to that first day, but none of my other ideas—slashing his tires, smashing his windshield, taking a bat to his precious Suburban—felt right either. I needed something more personal. I wanted him to know it was me.

After an hour or so, Derek left the house. I wasn't able to make a U-turn in time to catch up. I considered going by the club to see if his car was there, but my shoulder was starting to hurt, the roads were getting bad, and I wanted to be back at the apartment in time for the eleven-o'clock news.

Ted and I ended up getting thirty seconds or so at the end of the weather report, the feel-good story in a local traffic roundup. The reporter described me as wanting to avoid the limelight. Ted said he never saw the pickup coming. Rachel said, "He saved my son's life." I was on the sofa with the Chairman, trying to ignore the stiffness in my shoulder. I raised my can to the TV as best I could.

The next morning, I was in pretty sad shape for sledding. I could barely brush my teeth, and my hip ached. I bundled up, slowly, and went for Sara. She was out front in her snowsuit with Liz, who was dressed for work. They were watching three men unload chain saws and coils of rope from a truck in front of Clarice's. Behind the truck was a wood chipper.

"They're cutting Sicky down!" Sara wailed, running across the snowy yard and throwing her arms around me. "Make them stop!"

The workers were watching. I managed to pick her up, afraid she might try to stop them herself, and sat on the front steps. She was crying so hard she was hiccupping. Liz sat down next to us to stroke her hair. Clarice came outside in a long down coat and rubber boots. She spoke with the worker in charge, then crossed the street to tell Sara she'd be getting a new tree in the spring, a sapling, and Sara could help look after it. Sara didn't even acknowledge her.

"You said Sicky would be fine, Dad."

I was telling her the accident must have done more damage than I realized when Clarice interrupted.

"Actually, sugar," she said, "that tree was sick all along. I just didn't find out until I had somebody look at it after the crash."

Sara lifted her head from my shoulder. "You mean she isn't getting killed? She just died?"

"I'm sorry," Clarice said. "I wanted to wait until spring, but they're telling me I could have a problem if there's ice."

Sara asked if she could have a piece of the tree, and Clarice had one of the men cut her a branch the length of a walking stick. By then Liz had missed her train. She said she'd better get going or she'd miss the next one, too. Sara took her eyes off the tree crew just long enough to hug her good-bye, then told me she didn't feel like sledding anymore.

"I want to watch," she said.

I didn't think that was such a good idea: knowing what was happening and seeing it weren't the same. I was also still afraid she'd try to stop them. With the chain saws going, they might not notice her until it was too late. But she stayed put, sitting on the steps with her mittens on and the branch across her knees. We ended up watching them all morning. One of the guys climbed the tree with a chain saw, cutting limbs, while the others used rope pulleys to lower them to the ground. Once all the limbs were gone, the climber started working his way back down, roping and cutting sections of the trunk as he went. Sara said it reminded her of a candle burning down. Maybe she was thinking of the vigil; the crew was piling branches on the grass where the mourners had stood. The cross and flowers were on Clarice's front porch.

Despite what I'd told Tawana—that I couldn't stand the sight of that tree—I was sorry to see it go. Sara and I might not have been sitting there, alive, if not for its stopping Juwan's car. I put my good arm around her and asked if she was warm enough. She nodded and leaned into me. Later, when the men started feeding limbs into the chipper, she covered her ears and said she'd had enough.

Sara cheered up a little when a new bicycle decorated with a big pink bow arrived that afternoon, a present from Ted's family, and when I got back to my building, a huge gift basket was waiting in the manager's office.

"Call me if you need any help with the Cristal," he said, handing it over.

There was also a cabernet, a chardonnay, caviar, cheese, olives, chocolates, cookies, a grilled artichoke antipasto, and a thank-you card from Ted's parents that I stood on my dresser.

I was putting everything else back into the basket when Liz called, nearly hyperventilating. "I just saw Tawana."

She'd been out shoveling when Tawana showed up to put the memorial back together.

"She wanted to know why we wouldn't let Sara talk to the police. What was I supposed to say? I almost told her to call *you*." Instead, she'd given her our line about not wanting to put Sara through any more than we already had. "She was like, 'Any more *what*? All he wants to do is ask her some questions.' It was awful."

"Do you think he put her up to it?"

"No, I think she just wants the whole thing to be over. She said the autopsy report came back a few days ago. He was *twice* the legal limit. And still Rizzo won't close the case. He tells her he hasn't ruled out, quote unquote, further criminal wrongdoing. She said she dreads his calls. She was practically pleading."

I told Liz I was sorry. I said the investigation was my problem, not hers. "Next time just tell her it was my decision. Tell her to come see me."

"I hate this," Liz said. "I hate being like this. Her son's dead, and I'm standing there worrying about getting sued."

* * *

Sitting across the street from Derek's that night, I popped the cork on the Cristal—probably the most expensive champagne I'll ever have—and gulped it warm, straight from the bottle. I didn't deserve to savor it. More to the point, I wanted to blot Tawana from my thoughts as soon as possible. I couldn't stop imagining what it must have been like when Rizzo called. Being forced, again and again, to contemplate the accident, to wonder how many seconds of terror or pain Juwan had endured, if he'd really been alive before the medics arrived, if he'd known he was dying, if he'd thought of her. And for what? I pictured her hanging up, standing alone in the kitchen of that big house, listening for sounds that weren't there anymore—Juwan coming home from school, Juwan playing video games with his friends, Juwan on his skateboard in the empty swimming pool out back.

I took another swig of champagne and tried to concentrate on Derek. Him I could at least do something about. He was inside watching TV with the girl from the nightclub. They had a bowl of popcorn, cans of beer. After a while, he aimed the remote, and she got up for a couple more. I didn't like her being there. Watching them together made me feel like a creep, but that wasn't all. Seeing her stretch her legs across his, I longed for a similar night with Liz—a different life altogether—my *real* life—were it not for Derek. Maybe I couldn't blame him for the accident, but if I'd been a bomb waiting to go off that day, he was the one who'd lit the fuse. He was the one who'd *made* me a bomb in the first place.

By the time I'd polished off half the bottle, my hip was hurting. I had a bruise the size of a salad plate. Derek glanced up from the TV as I was shifting around, trying to get comfortable. He came and stood at the window. I thought he was looking right at me, and I looked right back. I hoped he recognized my car. I hoped I was making him uneasy. When he drew the curtains, it felt like a small victory. Driving home, one arm cradled in my lap, it occurred to me that maybe this was all I needed to be doing—getting inside his head, keeping him on guard. A few months of that would take a toll on anyone.

On Saturday, after my head cleared from too much champagne, Sara and I went to dinner and *The Nutcracker*. She brought along the branch, which she carried as tenderly as she would have a doll, and asked me to take her over to the memorial when we got home. Figuring Tawana wouldn't be stopping by to tend the flowers that late, I held Sara's hand and crossed the street. Clarice's house looked naked without the sycamore out front. The flowers now ringed the cross, which stood in a patch of wood chips where the workers had ground the stump. It pleased me, the more I thought about it, that the accident hadn't had anything to do with the tree coming down; I liked the idea that cause and effect wasn't always as simple as it seemed. Sara picked up a handful of wood chips, breathed in their smell, let them fall through her fingers.

"I know it's sad," I said, "but look at all these." Up and down the block, tall sycamores lined the street, their limbs forming a high canopy.

"They're not Sicky," she said.

By now Liz had come out onto the porch. I think she was still shaken from her conversation with Tawana—resenting me for it. She hardly spoke a word when I brought Sara to the door.

No lights were on at Derek's. I parked and reached under my seat for what was left of the Cristal. When the bottle was done and he still wasn't home, I began to worry he'd left town for the holidays.

The Suburban was back the next night, though. He had a Christmas tree up in the front window, and colored lights around his porch posts. Not long after I got there, he opened the front door and stepped out. I started the car and drove away, then returned ten minutes later. He came out again. This time he pulled the door shut behind him. He started toward me, cutting across the small yard. I waited until he was almost at the curb before I glided away. He turned and went for the Suburban, but I was gone before he ever got out of the driveway.

* * *

And then it was Christmas Eve. Sara brought over a box of ornaments and we decorated the tree, taking turns choosing Christmas songs on the computer. When we were done, she said it still looked bare, so we strung a bunch of popcorn. Then we opened presents. I'd gotten her a few books, some doll clothes, and pink roller skates. She'd made me a picture frame, hand-painted and decorated with fabric-and-button flowers. The photo was her on Santa's lap. Liz had taken her to see him at the mall that weekend, something we did every year, only this time I hadn't been there. When I told her how much I liked it, I had tears in my eyes. She said Liz had cried, too, when they'd had the picture taken.

"You're just growing up so fast."

We settled in with one of her new books, *Guinness World Records*—she was fascinated by the three-foot-long finger-nails, as I'd known she would be—and proceeded to sample everything in the gift basket. No matter how hard we tried, though, there was no forgetting where we were.

"Can't you come over tomorrow," she said, "just for a little while? Please?"

———

That wasn't the only time I came close to telling you our being apart was all your mom's idea. She claimed she was doing it for you, but I knew you wouldn't have wanted her to. I knew you would have asked her to stop. But in telling you, I'd have been using you, pitting you against her, and that wasn't something I was willing to do. I've wondered, though, if she might have listened to you. And if the ends would have justified the means.

———————

After Liz picked Sara up, the apartment felt emptier than ever. I put the Christmas music back on, opened a beer, and started gathering the wrapping paper strewn across the floor. I picked at what was left of the gift basket. I took a length of popcorn off the tree and dangled it for the Chairman to chase. I wrapped the necklace I'd bought for Liz—a delicate silver one from her favorite boutique in Maplewood. She'd said no presents, so I planned on giving it to her when we got back together. I wanted to have gifts for all the holidays we'd missed.

When it got dark, I thought about going to Derek's, but all day I'd been worrying that I was getting carried away. This was a guy with a gun, after all. What if some night he were waiting for me in the Suburban, or snuck around from behind the house? For that matter, what if he called the police?

The pub seemed as good a place as any to think it over. And it turned out I wasn't the only one with nowhere better to be. I ordered a pint and stood near the crowded bar, waiting for a stool. Dan was wearing a Santa hat. The Grinch was on TV. Now and then, someone in the crowd would boo him. I didn't talk to anyone, but it was a comfort having people around. I was still waiting for a seat when somebody clapped me on the shoulder.

"Well, well," Rizzo said. "If it isn't the crosswalk hero."

I felt as though a trapdoor had swung open at my feet. For all the time I'd spent anticipating this moment, seeing him was still a surprise. I could only assume he'd followed me, or been waiting for me, and now, finally, he was going to arrest me, having timed it so I could wake in jail on Christmas morning.

Then I got a look at him. His eyes were glassy. He took a clumsy step backwards as he held up two fingers for Dan. "One for me," he said, "one for the hero."

I turned to leave, but he grabbed my arm, the sore one, and smiled when he saw me wince.

"Everything okay there, Detective?" Dan said, glancing over from the tap.

"Old friends." Releasing my arm, Rizzo nodded to a table in the corner where he'd been sitting. I considered walking out, but I figured he'd follow me. The last thing I wanted was to be alone with him. I sat down. A waitress brought two beers. Rizzo clinked his against mine.

"Look at us," he said. "Christmas Eve, two divorced guys, all by our lonesomes. We could start a club."

"I'm not divorced." I handed him Linda Schwartz's card. "I have nothing to say to you."

"Finally lawyer up?" He tucked the card into his pocket without looking at it. "Well, I hate to disappoint, Mr.

Bauer, but the prosecutor, in his infinite wisdom, feels we don't have enough to bring charges. Especially now, with the autopsy."

He clinked his glass against mine again, too hard, and took a long swallow. I stared at the beer he'd sloshed onto the table, feeling not as relieved as I might have expected and wondering if this was just another of his mind games. So they weren't going to arrest me. That was something— supposing it was true. But what about closing the case?

Beer had begun dripping onto the floor. I tried to scoot back from the table, but the wall was in the way.

"I have to be somewhere," I said.

"Running out on me? After I bring such good tidings?" He shook his head. "No, sir, no can do. Got something to show you first." There was a basket of pretzels on the table. He took two and arranged them between us. "You," he said, pointing at one, "and him. Beer glass is the tree." He slowly moved the pretzels toward one another, reenacting the accident more or less as it had happened, including, of course, my cutting into and out of the other lane. I held my breath as he flipped Juwan's pretzel, tapped it against the glass, then closed his hand on it.

"Pretty good, huh?" he said. "Only question is, did you do it on purpose? I got a theory on that too."

He opened his hand and ate a piece of the broken pretzel. My stomach was tight as a fist.

"Long as I got the floor," he said, "long as I'm talking out of school, here's a little secret about confessions. Ever wonder why a guy owns up to something when it's only going to get him into trouble?" He held out a piece of the pretzel, shrugged when I didn't take it, ate it himself. "No need to knock yourself out guessing, Mr. Bauer. I'll just tell you. It's *stress*. That's what does it every time, good old-fashioned stress."

As he began to catalogue the various sources of that stress—guilt, regret, shame, anxiety—and detail their psychological and physiological effects, I searched the bar for a familiar face, anybody I might latch onto. But Dan was busy with customers, the waitress had disappeared, and the closest tables were all college kids, oblivious to us.

". . . and sooner or later," he was saying, "for most people, it gets to be too much. Sooner or later they confess. But not you, Mr. Bauer. You apparently have no conscience! It's like you're broke inside. Which is interesting to me, as a student of human nature. Usually you only get that with your hardened criminals."

He narrowed his eyes at me, like the answer to some important question might be faintly etched on my forehead. Then he leaned forward, lowering his voice. "Look, Glen— mind if I call you Glen?—I don't think you're a bad guy for what you did. A vehicular homicide, hey, that can happen to anyone. We're all of us just a rough day or a wrong move away from fuck all." He pushed his glass aside and leaned closer. "No, what makes *you* a bad guy is not owning up to it. Not letting those people get the justice they deserve, even if all that justice is, is you walk."

I put five dollars on the table. My voice cracked when I spoke. "She wants you to close the case," I said. "She wants it to be over."

Rizzo whistled. "How noble of you. How lucky she is to have you on her side."

He opened his wallet, but instead of taking the money, he brought out a photo and held it up. Juwan at around Sara's age, blue sweater vest over a white oxford, missing a front tooth just like she was. A school picture. I could imagine Rizzo calling Tawana, encouraging her to sue, offering his full cooperation. I glanced away, but still he held it there, trying to make me look, until finally he reached over, tucked it into my shirt pocket, and patted my chest.

I got up, not caring if he followed me out. I would have run if I'd had to. But he just swiveled to let me by.

"Like I was saying, though," he said, toasting me again, "nice job saving that kid. Merry Christmas to you and yours."

Outside, I started to throw the photo in the trash but stopped when I noticed handwriting on the back—Juwan's name, in a child's overly deliberate script. It had probably been intended for a classmate, just as Sara and her friends swapped school pictures. Wishing I'd left it on the table, I slid it back into my pocket and tried to forget about him, but there was no escaping what Rizzo had said. I walked away from the bar feeling as if I were under a spotlight. It followed me down the street to the apartment building, around back to the parking lot. It shone into my car as I headed toward Derek's. It beat down on me as I opened two warm cans of beer from the console, one after the other, and drank them as fast as I could, trying to keep my mind blank. With every breath I took, I could feel the photo in my pocket. I remember wishing I could show Derek and make him understand he'd been part of a chain of events that had led to a boy's death. Why should he get to go through life not knowing? But of course he wouldn't have given a shit, wouldn't have seen the connection. To him it would have been meaningless talk.

When I got to his house, I did what I should have done in the first place. I called the police. I told them a man had threatened me with a gun and gave them his address. I figured they could make more trouble for him than I ever might hope to, and now that I was apart from Liz and Sara, I no longer cared if he found out who I was and where I lived.

They were there in no time, five or six cars with their lights and sirens going. I was waiting on the sidewalk in front of the house. Derek appeared at the window, next to the Christmas tree.

"That guy right there," I said to the first two officers I saw.

As Derek came out onto the porch, both of them drew their guns and shouted for him to stop where he was and put his hands on his head. Other officers were taking up positions behind their cars.

"What the hell's going on?" Derek said, raising his hands. "This is my house."

They brought him out onto the sidewalk and began patting him down. He was wearing his usual track suit, this one Nike, red with white stripes.

"That's the guy you should be frisking," he said, looking over at me.

A couple of officers took our IDs, then asked what was going on. I told them what had happened on Thomas Boulevard. They were confused. They wanted to know why I was reporting it *now*, after all this time.

I said I hadn't gotten his license plate number. "But then tonight, I was driving by, and I saw his truck in the driveway. I recognized the four wheels in back."

"Lying bitch," Derek said. "He's out here every night. Just sits over there in his car."

By now, the other officers had put away their guns and were standing around watching. The two officers questioning us exchanged a look. They asked Derek if what I was saying was true.

"I don't know nothing about no gun," he said. "But yeah, we had a little run-in. Guy gave me the finger. I go over to see what for and he tells me he was flipping off some cop."

The taller cop cut me a smirk.

"Do you own a handgun, Mr. Dye?" the other one said.

He shook his head. "Like I said, I don't know nothing about no gun."

"Search his truck," I said, surer than ever the gun wasn't legal.

Derek smiled, took out his keys, and pressed a button. The Suburban's lights flashed. "Be my guest."

But they wouldn't do it—no warrant, no probable cause. They were ready for this to be over. I'd called them out for nothing.

"How about *his* car?" Derek said. "I'm thinking our man here has had a few. Might have a bottle in there."

The officers had had enough, though. One went to answer the radio in his car while the other handed back our licenses. He apologized to Derek for disturbing him on Christmas Eve and thanked him for his cooperation. Then he told me 911 was strictly for emergencies and that I was lucky not to be getting a citation.

"Now get out of here," he said. "Vacate the premises."

I crossed the street. The other officer was still in his car, filling out paperwork. The rest were leaving or gone. I stopped short when I got a look at his profile, but it was a moment or two before it dawned on me why he seemed familiar. For all I knew, he was the same officer who'd run the light on Thomas Boulevard. Not likely, to be sure, but the possibility unnerved me. He glanced up from his clipboard and cracked the window.

"What?"

* * *

163

I drove around until the police were gone, pounding another beer, then parked in front of Derek's house and headed up the walk. I was counting on his still not having the gun on him. He opened the door before I could knock.

"Get the fuck out of here, motherfucker," he said.

I swung as hard as I could, with my good arm. Even with two good arms, I wouldn't have had a chance against him, but I didn't care. All that mattered was hitting him. I missed his nose and got his mouth instead—his teeth. It felt like I'd put my fist into a grinder. I didn't have time to swing again. He hit me square in the jaw, once. The porch sprang up, slamming into my body. Everything began to spin. I fully intended to hit him again, but I was barely onto my hands and knees, reaching for a plastic chair for balance, when he kicked me in the ribs. That knocked the wind out of me. I fell off the porch, got hung up in some shrubs, then collapsed onto the snow-covered grass, desperate for even the smallest breath of air. I couldn't see him anymore, but I could hear him coming down the steps—taking his time, it seemed. The world had become a vacuum. I gasped for air again and gagged on a mouthful of blood. Then I heard his girlfriend shouting for him to stop. He was standing over me now.

"Dude must have a death wish." He touched a finger to the blood at the corner of his mouth, then took out his phone and called the police. He told them he'd been attacked, for no reason, by a stranger at his home. I wanted to say bullshit, I had reasons, but my jaw was numb. After a few tries, I got my feet under me again. He was still on the phone.

"Honey," his girlfriend said. "He's right behind you."

I meant to hit him as he was turning around, but all I managed was a handful of velour and a shove. It was like trying to shove a refrigerator. He brushed my hand away and let me fall. This time being on the ground was all right. The snow felt good against my face. Derek pulled his foot back like he was going to kick me again, then laughed. I just lay there, wondering as I had so many times before if Juwan ever knew what hit him.

Riding in the ambulance, it began to sink in, what could have happened to me back at his house. Imagining Sara and Liz getting the news, I slammed my head against the gurney again and again until the medics strapped me down and threatened to give me a tranquilizer. In the emergency room, at St. Barnabas, they put me on painkillers, bandaged my knuckles, stanched the bleeding in my mouth, and gave me a towel to help with the drooling. I was in and out the whole time. The X-rays showed a broken hand, fractured lower jaw, cracked ribs. Even with the medicine, my chest felt like it was full of hot coals that flared with every breath.

They called Liz, though I had asked them not to. She got there a little after midnight. I was still in the ER, propped up in bed. I looked away as she came in, not wanting to see the expression on her face when she saw mine.

"Jesus, Glen," she said. "Are you okay?"

It was hard to speak without moving my jaw. "I'll be fine. I got beat up."

"Beat up? By who? I thought you were in a wreck." She sat down next to the bed and pressed my hand between hers.

"Tell you later," I said. "I'm okay. Go home."

She wanted to know more, but I didn't know where to start, and the medicine was making me drowsy. She went to find a doctor. I drifted off. A little later, she woke me to say they'd be transferring me to the ICU. They wanted to run more tests and keep me under observation. Internal injuries were a possibility. It was almost 2 a.m. She said she'd come back in a few hours, after Sara finished opening her presents.

"She'll want to see you."

"Not like this," I said. "Not on Christmas."

"Then what should I tell her?"

"Tell her the truth." It came out sounding like *truce*. "Tell her I got beat up."

"I'll tell her you fell down the stairs."

The orthopedist who fitted my splint later that morning said I had what was known as a boxer's fracture, a break at the base of the small finger, on my left hand. "But 'brawler's fracture' is more like it," he said. "Boxers take precautions."

"Where's my wedding band?"

"Your hand was too swollen. It was either cut the ring or lose the finger."

The splint encased my pinkie and ring finger, leaving the others free. He told me my hand would be almost as good as new in twelve weeks. Same for my ribs, if not sooner, but in the meantime there was nothing he could do for them; they had to heal on their own. There was no orthodontist around to examine my jaw—not on Christmas—but my teeth still lined up, which he said was a good sign. Probably I could get by without screws and plates, though I might need my jaw wired shut for a few weeks, and then something called arch bars. He referred me to an oral surgeon. He wrote a prescription for more painkillers. He set my wedding band on the bedside table and said he hoped I liked soup and smoothies, because that's what I'd be eating for the next month.

Liz arrived as he was leaving, bundled up, wearing a knotty red scarf Sara had knitted with Helen's help. She looked worn out. She'd brought a sweatshirt and some old jeans of mine from the house so I wouldn't have to wear the clothes I'd arrived in, which were caked with dirt and dried blood.

"How was Christmas?" I said.

"Sara cried when I wouldn't let her come. She says you should use the elevator from now on. Did you know there's a police officer here?"

He'd been waiting in the hall while I was with the doctor. Now he knocked and introduced himself as Sergeant Miller. I recognized him from Derek's, not the officer I might have flipped off but the other one. He said he needed to get my side of things for the incident report. I didn't want Liz knowing what had happened, but I couldn't very well ask her to leave, so I told him it hurt to talk. "Call you tomorrow?"

He said he hadn't come all that way for nothing. "So let's get this over with."

My jaw was so swollen, I could actually see it. I checked with my free fingers to make sure I wasn't drooling, then proceeded to confirm what he already knew, that after they'd left, I had returned to the house and assaulted Derek.

"Wait a minute," Liz said. "You assaulted *him*?"

Miller said I was lucky. Derek wasn't pressing charges, provided I kept my distance. "He says you've been stalking him. Watching his house at night."

Liz put a hand on my thigh. "Let's stop right here and call your lawyer."

"His girlfriend corroborated his statement," Miller said.

"He threatened me with a gun," I said, moving my mouth as little as possible. "He should be locked up."

"All due respect," Miller said, "so should you." Having gotten what he needed, he stood to go. "The impound lot's closed today, but you can pick your car up tomorrow."

Liz waited until he was gone, then pulled a chair alongside the bed. "A gun?" she said. "What is wrong with you, Glen? What are you doing?"

I looked over at my wedding band, which was now shaped like the letter C, and began to explain that I'd been involved in a road rage incident. The other guy—*this* guy—had flown off the handle, accosted me, flashed a pistol.

"I'd have told you," I said, "but I didn't want to upset you."

"Too late for that."

She got up and stood at the window with her arms crossed. The snow was coming down again. The scrape of a plow reached us from across the parking lot. I tried to sit up, but my ribs wouldn't let me.

"Anyway, I was out for a drive last night and happened to see his truck. I called the police, but they didn't do anything."

"So naturally you attacked him."

"He's not going to sue me. I didn't do enough damage."

There was fury in her eyes when she turned around. "You think I care about that?" She said I was lucky I wasn't paralyzed, or brain damaged—lucky just to be alive. "You have a family, remember? Do you ever stop to think about us?"

I reached out to touch her, but she drew back. She said she felt like she only ever got half the story from me anymore. When and where, for instance, did all of this happen? Why exactly did the guy fly off the handle? What did I mean "flashed a pistol"? And what was I doing driving around Montclair on Christmas Eve?

"It's the same with the accident," she said. "Always dribs and drabs. After I saw Tawana the other day? Sara told me what happened outside the lawyer's office. So as far as I can tell, you almost got into not one but *two* accidents with Juwan, but for some reason you didn't want anybody to know."

I stared at my chest and concentrated on taking shallow breaths. I couldn't bring myself to call Sara a liar again. "I didn't want the police to think I might have been trying to get back at him."

She thought this over, biting her lip. "Okay. That makes sense. Don't give them a motive. I can see that. But how am I supposed to be on your side if you won't tell me these things in the first place?"

She was right. And sooner or later she was going to find out more.

"Also," I said, "with the gun—Sara was in the car. It happened on the way home from school, on the day of the accident."

In a few minutes, Liz would help me get dressed and drive me back to the apartment. On the way, I'd consider telling her that the prosecutor had decided not to charge me. But in the end, I wouldn't bring it up. We'd ride in silence. Snow would blow across the road in gusts, covering the lane lines. She'd pull into the handicapped space at the back of the building so I wouldn't have far to walk and tell me to call her if I needed anything. I'd lean over to kiss her, in spite of the pain, and then she'd reach across the seat and pull the door shut.

For now, though, we were still together in that hospital room, and I was still holding out hope that she'd take me back. But her expression had changed. She was looking at me like she didn't know who I was anymore. I assume she was imagining what might have happened to Sara if that gun had gone off, and I assume she was thinking, correctly, that the whole thing must have somehow been my fault, or else why hadn't I been more forthcoming to begin with? The problem, of course, was that every time I opened my mouth to tell her something, I only ended up revealing how much I'd been hiding.

"Should I come back?"

The attending physician was standing in the doorway with a clipboard to his chest. Liz turned to the window. I went ahead and invited him in, asking what exactly I had to do in order to go home.

Two days later, I was back at St. Barnabas, having my jaw wired shut. For five weeks I ate from a blender and talked through my teeth, all the while debating whether to go ahead and tell Liz everything once and for all. I didn't think it would get me home any sooner, but I was afraid that if I didn't come clean, we might be done for. Things hadn't been the same between us since the hospital. She didn't have to say anything; I could see it in her eyes every afternoon when I dropped Sara off, moving like a broken old man. *You have a family, remember? Do you ever stop to think about us?*

At the end of January, my splint came off just as the first W2s were rolling in. The next three months were a welcome blur of work, ten- and twelve- and then fourteen-hour days that left time for little else except sleep and afternoons with Sara. I wouldn't say I was able to put my troubles out of mind, not even for a little while, but the nonstop emails and meetings and filings made it easier to get through the days.

By the time I came up for air, toward the end of April, I'd realized what a bad idea confessing to Liz would be. The moment for that had long since passed; honesty for honesty's sake wasn't going to win me any points at that late date. I could no more undo lying to her than I could undo the accident itself, and telling the truth now would only confirm her darkest suspicions—not just about how much I'd kept from her but also about my judgment. She'd never be able to forgive Juwan's death, and in her eyes that wouldn't even be the worst of it—it would always be secondary to the danger I'd put Sara in by cutting the wheel on purpose.

Another idea had occurred to me, though, one that seemed to have the potential to solve at least some of our problems: What if we went ahead with a divorce, and then I moved home? We'd live together as an unmarried couple. Since we'd officially be divorced, she wouldn't have to worry about a lawsuit. It was that simple. And who would even know? I didn't see why we'd have to go into the details with Sara or anybody else; we'd just say we were getting back together.

The prospect of a divorce still turned my stomach, but it was nothing compared to the prospect of more time apart. That winter and spring, in addition to the distance between me and Liz, I'd started to feel Sara slipping away. We'd go out to a diner for a busted-jaw special, mashed potatoes and milkshakes, and she'd make it through the whole meal without any of the sadness she'd shown before Christmas. She no longer clung to me when I dropped her off each night. She'd stopped asking when I was coming home. Our arrangement was starting to seem normal to her.

I made my proposal to Liz at the beginning of May, when I stopped by the house to give her a check. We were standing on the front porch, which was where we had most of our conversations. The lilacs were just starting to bloom, and I wondered if she remembered all the times she'd taken my hand and led me to the bushes to bury our faces in the purple blooms, inhaling their fragrance.

"It's not as crazy as it sounds," I said. "I talked to Schwartz. There's no law against divorced couples living to-gether." I said I was ready to sign the papers and move home anytime. I said I knew we had a lot to work out, but it wasn't likely to happen with us separated, so why not give it a try under one roof?

At first she thought I was joking, or pretended to. She

said she wasn't even going to run that one past Braun. "If we ever did get sued, don't you think it would be a little transparent?"

"Liz, please," I said, trying not to sound as frustrated as I felt. "The accident was six months ago. You know that's not going to happen."

"Don't tell me what I know."

I searched her eyes, but she was staring off across the street. A sapling now stood where the sycamore had been. The cross was still there, and flowers, though fewer than before.

"I'm sorry," she said. "I can't be with someone I can't trust."

Though I wasn't entirely surprised to hear the words, still they hit me like a door slamming shut. Ten years of marriage, gone just like that, and I couldn't even pinpoint when exactly I'd lost her for good. I took her hand and told her I loved her and couldn't imagine living without her. I said we should stay together for Sara's sake if nothing else. I asked if she'd at least consider counseling, which was something Schwartz had suggested.

"That would make it look like we're trying to get back together," she said.

"But what about our *real* marriage?"

Her hand was limp in mine. "This is the only marriage we've got."

*   *   *

A few days later, Liz told me she'd asked Sara about Derek Dye. Apparently Sara remembered our encounter with him well. She told Liz he'd accused me of giving him the finger but that she hadn't seen me do it. That was enough for Liz, though. Another secret I'd kept from her, another example of my recklessness. She informed me she was going ahead with a divorce.

"A real one," she said.

We argued. I said quitting on our marriage was one thing, but how could she possibly justify trying to take Sara away from her father?

"You always said you'd do what's best for her," I said. "No matter what."

She said that's exactly what she was doing—that she could no longer trust me to exercise the most basic kind of parental good judgment, that if I'd put Sara in harm's way once, I'd do it again. She said she had no intention of coming between us but that Sara was her life, and she wanted to be the one calling the shots now that she couldn't count on me. I suggested slowing down—in less than a year, if she still wanted to, we'd be able to file for a no-fault divorce—but she said she wasn't going to change her mind, and she wasn't going to wait.

We got the lawyers involved. I admit, I was as much to blame as she was. I knew I didn't have a chance, knew I'd lost her and our marriage and that it was my own doing, but I fought her for Sara all the way. It wasn't so different from hurling myself at Derek, only this time I had plenty of opportunities to reconsider, plenty of chances to pull back before the day came that Sara was standing in front of the mediator, being asked whom she'd rather live with, refusing to give him any answer except "Both of them."

———————

Once the papers were signed and it was official, I was afraid she'd make things hard on me, but here it is, almost a year later, and your mom has been true to her word. She has never tried to keep us apart. If anything, she's gone out of her way to make sure we have time together.

Not that you initially wanted much time with either of us. Remember? It was months before you stopped threatening to teach us a lesson and run away from home. You also said we should stop apologizing, because if we were really, truly sorry for what we'd done, we wouldn't have done it, or we'd undo it.

You had a point. Nothing we'd done, after all, was inevitable. I'd made mistakes, she'd made mistakes, and we'd ended up in a place I don't think either of us ever envisioned. It seemed like we should have been able to say, "Oops, we got carried away, let's start over," but of course it doesn't work that way.

I am really, truly sorry, though, and I'll probably still be apologizing when you read this ten years from now.

———————

A couple of weeks after the statute of limitations expired, I overheard Sara in the school yard explaining to a friend that the reason her parents split up wasn't that they didn't love each other, it was because of a car crash. I stood and stared, too stunned to move. In the two years since the accident, I'd never heard her say such a thing. Certainly she hadn't gotten it from me or Liz. We'd explained the divorce simply by saying we couldn't get along anymore—something that sometimes happened to grown-ups, we'd said, even ones who still cared about each other. No, Sara had come up with this on her own. Now she noticed me watching and quickly turned away, instructing her friend not to tell anyone.

"It's a secret."

On the drive home, she said she didn't want to talk about it, she hadn't been talking to me, I shouldn't have been eavesdropping.

"But I don't understand," I said. "Why would you think the accident had anything to do with the divorce?"

I didn't think she was going to answer, and for a good ten minutes, she didn't, just sat in silence, staring out the window. A few blocks from the apartment, though, she suddenly said she didn't know why, that's just how she remembered it.

"You and Mom got along fine until the accident, and then you started fighting."

"About what, exactly?"

"About whether it was your fault."

We were stopped at a light on Scotland Road. Composing myself, I turned until I felt the twinge in my ribs that has never gone away. "I don't remember us fighting about that," I said, "but you're right about the timing. That's when we started having trouble getting along." I turned back to the road so she couldn't see my face. "Do *you* think it was my fault?"

She drummed her feet against the back of the passenger seat. The light changed. We turned onto West Montrose, then Vose. "Not if you didn't mean to," she said, finally. "You didn't mean to scare him."

My knuckles went white on the steering wheel. So there it was. She'd known all along, or at least suspected. Of course I'd meant to scare him. If she hadn't seen it in my eyes as I cut the wheel that day, watching me in the rearview mirror as she was watching me now, then it was only a matter of time before the full truth dawned on her.

"But you always said it was his fault," I reminded her. "You never said anything about me."

She resumed kicking the seat. "I know. I thought you'd be upset."

I called Liz and asked her to meet me for lunch in Millburn. She would have preferred someplace closer to home, but ever since the night with Rizzo, I'd avoided South Orange's shops and restaurants. We got the last sidewalk table at a little Mexican place on the main drag, its entrance decorated with skulls and orange marigolds for the Day of the Dead. After we ordered and made plans to meet for Sara's parent-teacher conference, I told her what Sara had said to her friend on the playground and what she'd said to me. Liz was as surprised as I'd been.

"Thank God we never let her talk to Rizzo," she said.

Trails of red leaves swirled in the traffic, catching sunlight as they sifted onto the sidewalk. It was the sort of glorious autumn day that will always remind me of the accident. But I told Liz it was time—more than time—to be putting the accident behind us. It had been two years. We should have been getting on with our lives. "What would you think about moving?" I said. After all, we'd come to New Jersey for a job she no longer had. Why stay in that house, on that street, with all those memories? We were both self-employed; we could go anywhere we wanted. "You pick a place. I'll follow you."

She pointed out that she couldn't go just anywhere because most of her clients were in the city. "Besides, I don't want Sara having to switch schools."

"Then how about just to another town?" I said. "Someplace closer to Montclair. No more fifty-minute trips." I started ticking off places that fit the bill—Bloomfield, Nutley, Verona, Montclair itself, if we could find something affordable—until she interrupted to say okay, it was a possibility, she'd think about it. She said she'd start by bring-

179

ing it up with Kim, whom Sara had continued to see after the divorce. Then she asked if I'd called about the autopsy lately. The medical examiner had never publicly released the report, so we could only assume the case was still open, technically at least. I'd resigned myself to this, knowing there was no statute of limitations for a criminal charge involving a death. And knowing that even if he wasn't actually working the case anymore, Rizzo would have wanted that hanging over my head.

"No," I said. "I'm done calling."

Which brings me to why I started this letter in the first place. Call it stress or remorse or whatever you like, but after our conversation in the car, I knew I had to tell you the truth, that I wouldn't be able to live with myself if I didn't. I hated the thought of you carrying around suspicions, wondering about me every time you looked over at Clarice's yard or saw me behind the wheel of a car.

At least that's how I felt in the beginning. Now that I've gotten it all out, though, I admit, I'm having second thoughts. Why tell you things that are only going to hurt us both? Why assume you'll eventually figure it out? Why not wait and see?

Maybe Rizzo was right. Maybe I am broken. Because if I felt as bad about the accident as I've always said I do, wouldn't I have confessed and faced whatever the consequences might be?

I originally wanted to tell you all of this in person, at whatever point in time I thought you were ready for it, but it occurred to me that I should write it down too, in case I'm not around when that time comes. My plan was to provide a copy to Linda Schwartz and make arrangements for you to get it when you turned eighteen. I figured this would also keep me from changing my mind. Already I'm anxious thinking about that day. You'll be the same age Juwan was when he died. I've tried to picture you then, whether your hair will have gotten darker and straighter like your mom's. Whether you'll have that skeptical look of hers that I've seen so much of. Whether you'll still call me Daddy.

I promised myself I wouldn't turn sentimental here at the end and go on about how much I love you. I wanted to close with something useful. A lesson you could apply to your own life. The problem is, I'm not sure what that might be. That it's a good idea to tell the truth? That actually it doesn't matter if you do? That sometimes your mistakes catch up with you and sometimes they don't? Or that they always do, though not necessarily in the ways you might expect?

Just this afternoon, as I was helping you with your homework, you started going through my wallet and pulled out the photo of Juwan that Rizzo gave me. Not long after I got beat up, I stopped by Tawana's, meaning to put the picture in the mailbox, but the house was empty, with a SOLD *sign out front. To just leave it there seemed wrong.*

What's this? you said, pointing to a stain on the photo. Blood, I said. His? you said. No, I said, mine. From when you fell down the stairs? you said. I nodded. You made a face, then took your own school photo from the wallet and laid them side by side. You asked why I had a picture of Juwan—which was a good question. It's not like I was stuck with it. I could have left it at the memorial. I could have thrown it out. Instead, for reasons I didn't fully understand, I'd chosen not only to keep it but to carry it with me. I figured I was doing it out of guilt and a sense of obligation. The truth didn't hit me until that moment, though, looking into your blue eyes.

To remind me to be careful, I said.

Acknowledgments

Having a book published—having the opportunity to be read—is an enormously humbling experience. I'm very glad for the chance to thank the people who made this one possible.

This book benefited greatly from the expertise and generous help of Arnold Anderson, S. Scott Haynes, Dr. William Vincent Burke, and Delvan Roehling. Thank you all for going above and beyond the call (and a belated thanks, Scott and Vince, for your invaluable help on the last book too).

On the publishing side, a huge thanks to Julie Barer, who I can always count on—working with you is a pleasure and a privilege—and to the good people at Free Press, most notably Wylie O'Sullivan, Martha Levin, Dominick Anfuso, Jill Siegel, Sydney Tanigawa, Sharbari Kamat, and Meghan Healey. Your collective faith and patience made all the difference.

I will always be deeply indebted to the faculty of the MFA program at Ohio State, especially Lee K. Abbott, Michelle Herman, and Erin McGraw; to the graduate creative writing students at Ohio State, circa 1992–1996 (you know who you are); to Mary Grimm at Case Western; to Dick and Lois Rosenthal; to the Squaw Valley Community of Writers; and to the Bread Loaf Writers' Conference, most recently for the friendship and fellowship (thanks, fellows) I enjoyed there in 2008.

Special thanks also to Jen Barrett, for your good eye and good humor.

On the home front, for your immeasurable support, thanks to Beth Cain, Richard and Joanne Way, Jennifer Way, and of course Jeff Weiser.

Last and best, I am most grateful to Deborah—always the reader I write for—without whose tireless editorial care and wisdom this book simply wouldn't be; and to Hazel—for listening, and for bringing such joy to my life. I love you both so.

What You Have Left

A Novel

Will Allison

"Remarkable. . . . One of the year's best fiction debuts."
— *Entertainment Weekly*

"In spare, transparent prose, Allison captures the truth and irony of being part of a family, no matter how broken it is."
— *The Washington Post*

"Allison gets at a mother's raw nerve, a father's desperate evasions, the daredevil rage of an abandoned daughter, and the anxiety of a husband curbing his own destructive impulses as he gauges the risks of love."
—*O, The Oprah Magazine*

CHAPTER ONE
1991
Holly

I was sentenced to life on my grandfather's dairy farm in the summer of 1976. The arrangement was supposed to be temporary, a month or so until my mother recovered from her water-skiing accident, but after one week, on the first day she was able to get out of her hospital bed and walk, a blood clot traveled up from her leg, blocked the vessels to her lungs, and killed her. My father had been the one driving the boat, the one who steered too close to the dock. Three days after the funeral, he walked out of the insurance agency where he worked and wasn't heard from again.

Though my grandfather, Cal, spent months trying to track him down, it was no use, and that's how, at the age of five, I came to be spending my nights in the bed my mother had slept in as a child. Cal made a gift to me of my mother's arrowhead collection, which he'd helped her assemble when she was little. He also decided to repaint her bedroom for me and said I could pick the color. He was trying to be nice, but I wasn't ready for nice. At Taylor Hardware, I chose Day-Glo orange, held the sample card up for my grandfather's approval, and then proceeded to pick out three more hideous shades of orange—one for each wall—daring him to say no. Instead of stopping me, instead of telling me one color would do, he'd simply nodded. "Anything you want, sugar plum," he said. Naturally, I threw a tantrum. What I wanted was my mom and dad, not stupid paint for a stupid room in a stupid old farmhouse. I'm sure everyone in the store thought I had it coming, but rather than drag me out to the parking lot for a spanking, as he'd surely have done with my mother, Cal just picked me up and held on as I kicked.

My grandfather's relationship with my mother, his only child, was a difficult one, and the subject of her death always left him at a loss. Whenever I asked about her, Cal would either fall silent or try to deflect my questions with anodyne bits of wisdom, mostly quotations from the tattered Bartlett's he kept by the toilet. His standby, the old chestnut that exasperated me most, was a line from Hubert Humphrey: "My friend, it's not what they take away from you that counts; it's what you do with what you have left."

At the time, of course, I was too young to appreciate what my grandfather was doing with what he had left—raising yours truly—and in all my worry over what had been taken from me, I failed to consider how much had been taken from him. My grandmother, Josie, had passed away before I was born, and shortly after my mother's death, my great-grandfather died as well. The Colonel had been living in the Alzheimer's ward of a nursing home in Blythewood, a low brick building that smelled of Pine-Sol and pea soup. I hated visiting him, but Cal always brought me along, telling me that one day I'd be glad I'd gotten to know my great-grandfather.

There wasn't much left to know. During our visits, the attendant would park the Colonel's wheelchair by the window, where the sunlight lent his eyes a misleading sparkle. On the rare occasions he addressed me, he called me by my mother's name, Maddy, but usually he'd just grab my wrist and shake it, moaning, oh oh oh. Looking back on those visits, I now see that if they were unpleasant for me, they were torture for Cal, who wasn't just seeing his father; he was seeing his own future self. Over the years, he'd watched his grandfather, his uncle, and now the Colonel succumb to the same disease—smart, willful men reduced to drooling and diapers. He'd seen the ugliness of it, the anvil weight on his family, and he was determined not to go down the same road. Driving home from the Colonel's funeral, he took a long swallow from his silver flask and swore he'd take matters into his own hands before it came to that.

I never forgot that vow, though when I was old enough to understand what it meant, I told myself it was just talk, that my grandfather would never intentionally leave me. But in the end, Cal was true to his word. When his mind started to go, he fought back with a handful of sleeping pills, leaving me the farm where I now live with my husband, Lyle, who was hired to renovate the farmhouse in the months before Cal's death.

My grandfather first told me he was sick during the spring of my sophomore year at Carolina. He was starting to slip, was how he put it. "Maybe it's something and maybe it's not," he said. "The doctors don't know for sure yet." It was early April, and I was at the farm for our weekly cocktails, the two of us sitting out front beneath the mossy live oaks, a pitcher of Cal's peppery bloody marys on the wrought-iron table between us. I watched Lyle and his crew stacking steel beams alongside the house as Cal told me that over the past few months, he'd begun forgetting things—names, appointments, the day of the week. He figured it was probably old age, no reason to get all bent out of shape, but just to be safe, he'd gone to the VA for a checkup. They'd given him a physical and a mental-status evaluation. Now they wanted him back for more tests. I stared into my drink, thinking about how he'd forgotten my birthday that fall, how I'd been so busy with classes and pledge meetings that I blew it off, even though it was exactly the sort of lapse I'd always been on the lookout for. Cal patted my knee and told me to cheer up. "Like Yogi Berra said, it ain't over till it's over." Then he stared into his drink, too. "Course, he also said the future ain't what it used to be."

The pecky-cypress paneling in the master bedroom of our house is pitted and scarred, the handiwork of a thousand woodpeckers, or at least that's what I imagined as a five-year-old. When I'd asked Cal about his funny-looking walls, though, he told me the pockmarks weren't the result of woodpeckers or worms or beetles, as many people believed, but rather a rare and little-understood fungus. "What makes pecky hard to find," he said, "is that you can't tell if a cypress is infected until you chop down the tree and cut it open."

When he'd purchased the farm, in 1939, the house wasn't a house, it was a grain barn. He divided the building into rooms and framed doors and windows using wood from an old sharecropper's cabin. After that first drafty winter, Josie shivering next to him in bed, he decided to insulate and panel their bedroom walls. He originally thought he'd get the wood from the Colonel's sawmill, but this was the Depression: Cal couldn't afford to buy lumber, and the Colonel couldn't afford to give it away, not even to his own son. The best he could do was let Cal help himself to the scrap pile, which was where he found, underneath an old tarp, a load of pecky cypress, enough to panel the bedroom and his workshop. In later years, people would develop a taste for pecky and an appreciation for its scarcity, but in those days, it was considered junk wood. Josie didn't care; she said it had low-country charm. Mainly, though, she was pleased that Cal went to all that trouble for her even as he worked twelve-hour days trying to establish their dairy farm. Her gratitude was not lost on him, and for the rest of her life, whenever he wanted to please her, he embarked on some new project to make the house more comfortable. Just before my mother was born, he added on a whole second story, and in later years he expanded the dining room and added a built-in china cabinet, then converted the front porch into a sitting parlor with French doors. In 1969, he was halfway done painting the house a minty shade of green that Josie picked out when doctors discovered the tumor in her breast.

After Josie's death, my grandfather let the house fall into disrepair, but during the fall of my sophomore year, when he first began having trouble with his memory, he sold off several parcels of land and started using the money to fix the place up. Though I didn't know it at the time, he did this for me, for when I inherited the farm.

At seventy-two, he was no longer able to do the work

himself, so he hired Lyle on the recommendation of an old army buddy. In those days, Lyle was more handyman than general contractor, but he worked cheap, and my grandfather liked his manners, the fact that his family was well off, the fact that he'd been smart enough for grad school but then turned his back on all that academic baloney. Inside a month, Cal was inviting him to join us for happy hour. By then I already had my eye on Lyle—a shirtless guy tuck-pointing a chimney apparently being one of my weaknesses—but he seemed more interested in Cal's company than mine, so I played it close to the chest.

That all changed on the afternoon my grandfather told me he was sick. He'd just finished filling me in on his visit to the VA when Lyle and the two guys who worked for him came crawling out from under the house, brushing soil from their jeans. That week they were trying to fix the sloping floor in the living room. The joists beneath the oak floorboards were supported by heavy girders cut from the heartwood of long-leaf pines, and their plan was to reinforce these girders with steel beams, jack them up, and then build concrete pillars to stabilize the floor. After his crew knocked off for the day, Lyle joined us and began to report on their progress, and soon talk turned to the next project, a new roof. My grandfather didn't mention his health again, but I could think of nothing else, and as he and Lyle droned on about shingles and soffits, I stared out at the fields that once fed Cal's registered Guernseys and quietly plowed my way through two more drinks.

When the sun started to dip behind the bluff, Cal left for his monthly poker game at the country club; as he drove down the lane, he flashed us the peace sign, something he'd picked up from Lyle. Once he was gone, I lit a smoke and emptied the last of the pitcher into my glass. "You ought to make sure he pays you before he blows his brains out," I said. Lyle smiled, then quit smiling when he saw I was serious, then smiled again because he didn't know what else to do.

"Come again?"

I sent him inside to mix another pitcher, and when he returned, I continued to get embarrassingly drunk and told him everything, all the while vaguely aware that I was trying to seduce him, never mind that he was twenty-four and I was only nineteen. When I got around to the part about Cal planning to "take matters into his own hands," Lyle was doubtful. "Isn't that just something people say? To give themselves a sense of control?"

"You don't know my grandfather," I said. I hoped Lyle was right, though. It had always terrified me to think Cal would end up like the Colonel, but even that would have been better than no Cal at all. Still, the few times he'd alluded to killing himself—usually in the fading twilight of a vodka-soaked cocktail hour, and usually in the context of what his father ought to have done—I'd simply nodded along, trying to maintain the sort of grown-up composure he admired. I understood, even as a child, that I was always being compared to my mother, contrary, contentious, confounding Maddy. "You," he'd say, tousling my hair, "you I don't have to worry about."

But of course he worried anyway, and as I sat there with Lyle, listening to the crickets and watching the Spanish moss flutter in the breeze, I began to understand why Cal kept inviting him to join us: He was worried about what would happen to me after he was gone. He was worried about me being alone. By now I'd started to get weepy, and Lyle put an arm around me, telling me things would work out. The fireflies were just starting to appear as I took his hand and led him into the house, through the French doors of the parlor, past the pocked paneling of the workshop, and upstairs to the bedroom with faded Day-Glo walls and the curio cabinet lined with my mother's arrowheads.

A few days before semester's end, Cal was scheduled for a neurological exam at the VA, but he missed the appointment. Dr. Miller assumed he'd forgotten—a symptomatic memory lapse—but I chalked it up to my grandfather's dislike of hospitals, and who could blame him, given the way things had turned out with Josie and my mother? It was decided that I'd take him to his next appointment. On a Tuesday morning in early May, I hurried through a biology exam and then drove out to the farm. When I arrived, I found Cal in his workshop, a stifling, narrow room crowded with fishing poles, hand tools, gardening tools, faded seed packets, scraps of sandpaper, bits of wood, rusted Folgers cans filled with nails, screws, washers, nuts, and bolts. He invited me in. On his workbench was a brown prescription bottle; he'd been grinding up pills with the porcelain mortar and pestle he'd once used to mix medicine for livestock. As he poured the powder back into the bottle, he said that if it turned out he was sick—and nobody was saying for sure he was, don't go burying him yet—but if he was, this was how he'd do it. Sleeping pills. Twenty of them dissolved in a stiff drink were guaranteed to do the trick. I picked up one of the bottles and examined the label, feeling suddenly hot and dizzy, as if I'd just downed a handful of pills myself.

"Why not just use a shotgun?"

"And mess up this pretty face?" Cal tapped his watch and turned to go: We didn't want to miss another appointment.

In spite of the tough-girl act I put on for Cal, I never could stomach what passed for mercy on a farm. Over the years, I saw him put down more animals than I care to remember: sick cows, sick goats, and sick chickens; rabbits maimed by cats, cats mauled by dogs, dogs hit by cars. "You don't let a suffering thing suffer," he'd say. One hazy morning when I was ten, I went to the mailbox and found our coon dog, Leopold, lying in a ditch beside the highway, bleeding from the mouth. His ribs quivered as if he were torn between the need for air and the pain of breathing. My grandfather brought his shotgun, took one look at Leo, and did what needed to be done. When I heard the gunshot, what I felt was relief, but also a kind of hatred.

Lyle stood in the middle of my grandfather's workshop admiring the pecky cypress while I rifled the shelves above the workbench. "You know what this stuff is worth?" he said, tracing a finger along the pale wood.

"He got it for free," I said. "Ask him. He loves to tell the story." When I didn't find what I was looking for on the shelves,

I checked the window to make sure Cal was still practicing his golf swing, then moved on to his tackle box. As I scanned the trays of iridescent flies, Lyle told me about a friend of his whose father once owned a lumber mill up in Spartanburg. He said that when they cut open a cypress and discovered it was pecky, they used to shut down the whole operation, drive that one tree to market, and split the profits. "Then they'd take the rest of the day off," he said. "All thanks to some worms."

The pill bottle was hidden among spools of fishing line in the bottom of the tackle box. I handed it to Lyle. He unscrewed the cap and looked inside, frowning. For a minute or two we just stood there, listening to the sounds of his crew tearing off the old roof, the hollow pop of Cal giving flight to another ball. Finally Lyle said, "So what are you going to do?" I'd been hoping he'd insist we talk to Cal, take away his pills, put him in a nursing home if that's what it took, but Lyle just stood there squinting in the hard light that slanted through the window, looking like he wished he were someplace else.

"You don't think I should do anything, do you?"

"I didn't say that," Lyle said. "But it is his life, right?"

I put the pill bottle back in the tackle box and pushed past him on my way out. He caught up with me in the kitchen pouring a shot of whiskey. When he started to apologize, I cut him off. "And the worms in pecky cypress?" I said. "Any idiot knows it's a fungus."

The neurological exam raised red flags, so the next week, I took Cal in for a dizzying alphabet of tests—EEG, CT,

MRI, PET, SPECT. Then it was back to the psychiatrist, this time for neuropsychological screening, a series of interviews and written tests that left Cal exhausted and irritable. Dr. Miller kept telling us it was a process of elimination; they had to rule out a thyroid problem, stroke, depression.

By the time it came, the diagnosis was no surprise. "Dementia," Dr. Miller said, "of the Alzheimer type." We were sitting in his office at the VA. Cal didn't even blink. "Of the type, huh? You sure you got the right type?" Dr. Miller understood that he was being mocked, but he kept his cool, explaining yet again that an educated guess was the best he could do.

I'd learned all about Alzheimer's in middle school, when I studied up on it in the school library. I read about the change that occurs in the brain, the formation of a mysterious, gummy plaque whose presence can be verified only by autopsy. It had made me think of our pecky cypress walls, and sometimes I imagined my grandfather dead on a conveyor belt, a buzz saw slicing into his head as curious lumberjacks leaned in for a look. Of course, whereas a pecky cypress shows no external signs of its illness, an Alzheimer's patient shows plenty, so I'd compiled a list of warning signs in my notebook—memory loss, difficulty performing familiar tasks, problems with language, changes in mood or behavior, etc. For years I watched my grandfather and waited, ready for doom every time he so much as misplaced his keys or confused the names of my friends.

And now that the dark clouds on the horizon had finally rolled in, I found myself facing an even worse wait.

The doctors told Cal he might last three years or he might last twenty, but Cal knew that in our family, the disease tended to hit hard and fast, and he seemed determined not to put things off. It made sense that he'd want to take care of business now, while he still had the presence of mind to do so. The day after he was diagnosed, he met with his lawyer about putting his affairs in order, and that weekend he made clear to me that he wanted to finish work on the house as soon as possible. "How soon?" I asked him. It was after the end of spring semester, a Saturday morning, and we were unloading boxes into the swaybacked barn that once sheltered his farming equipment—tractor, sickle mower, silage chopper, disc harrow, bottom plow. The cannibalized remains of an old combine still filled one corner, but the other machines were gone, sold at auction in 1977, the year Cal buried the Colonel and herded his cows between the milking parlor's stanchions for the last time.

"End of summer," he said. "Labor Day at the latest."

"That's not much time."

"Lyle'll manage," Cal said, lifting another box from the pickup and piling it onto a wooden pallet alongside the combine. We'd been clearing out the attic so Lyle's crew could add new insulation, and we were down to the last load, mostly boxes containing my mother's belongings. After my father skipped town, Cal had gone to the little lake house where we lived, packed her stuff, and stowed everything in the attic. As a child, I wasn't supposed to go up there—Cal told me there were bats—but that never stopped me. I'd spent hours going through her clothes, poring over her photo albums and scrapbooks. Now, rearranging the boxes on the pallet, my arms felt dead, like elastic bands that had lost their snap. Cal was tireless, though. His sun-leathered hands looked as if they could still wrestle a breech calf from a panicked heifer. While he went back to the truck, I took a breather, digging through a box until I found my mother's wedding dress in its plastic dry cleaner's bag. It was more sundress than wedding gown, a bit too Summer of Love for my taste, but as I held it against me and swished from side to side, I could see its appeal. When I glanced up, Cal was standing in the doorway of the barn, a wistful smile on his face. "You know, I never did think I'd see you in a wedding dress."

"And maybe you never will," I said. I was hoping to hurt him a little, to remind him what he had to live for, but Cal just seemed confused. He started to say something and then stopped, staring at me as if I were a familiar face he couldn't quite place. It wasn't until he turned back to the truck, clearly shaken, that I understood it wasn't me he'd been talking to.

I moved back to the farm the following weekend. Cal tried to talk me out of it, suggesting I stay put in the sorority house, but I said I wanted to spend more time with him, and he couldn't argue with that. For the first few weeks, life wasn't so different than it had been the previous summer. The doctors had fine-tuned Cal's medication, and it was possible, watching him peruse the newspaper or tie a fishing lure, to imagine his diagnosis had simply been wrong. Then June melted away into July, and the blast-furnace heat of midsummer seemed to slow everything down, including Cal. Simple conversation began to confound him, his thoughts like knotted rope, and twice he got lost driving in town, unable to solve the once-familiar streets. Determined not to embarrass himself, he gave up his poker game, turned down fishing trips, stopped answering the phone.

We continued our Friday cocktails against doctor's orders, but even with Lyle there, those evenings were strained. I'd never realized how much you talk about the future until the topic was off limits. With nowhere to be, Cal invariably ended up drunk. Lyle encouraged me to water down his drinks, but instead I poured him doubles, so he'd sleep sooner. By then I was spending two or three nights a week at Lyle's apartment, hurrying home each morning so I could have grits and toast waiting on the table for Cal. After breakfast, he'd spend a few hours doing whatever he could to help Lyle, but the afternoons were ours. When we finished lunch, usually leftover fried chicken or barbecue sandwiches bought for the workers, we'd head out to his makeshift driving range, a onetime soybean field he'd seeded with Kentucky bluegrass after he gave up farming. For years he'd been wanting to teach me golf; now I took him up on his offer. We'd start by walking the range together, gathering balls in an old milk pail, and then he'd coach me until the afternoon sun drove us inside, all the while fielding questions about my mother and Josie as I worked to keep his memory sharp. I wasn't really expecting to hear anything new, but after fifteen years of mostly dodging the subject, Cal surprised me by talking more frankly about his problems with my mother. In between pointed critiques of my grip and stance, he confessed to having been overly protective and overly strict, not letting my mother live her own life, as she used to say to him.

The trouble between Cal and my mother started when she came down with rheumatic fever. She was seven years old, and the doctor said she'd be crippled for life if her heart wasn't given sufficient time to heal. He ordered six weeks bed rest. She was not to get up at all—Cal and Josie would feed her, bathe her, change her clothes, even take her to the bathroom.

That was 1954, the summer Cal tore down the old barn and built a new one. One of the farmhands, Willie Jones, used to ferry my mother around on his shoulders while she was sick. Sometimes he'd set her on a blanket under the chinaberry tree so she could watch the barn rising in the field. The chief carpenter, Old Man Carey, carried a bar of Octagon soap in his pocket, and with the help of Cal's binoculars, she'd study the way he soaped each nail before driving it into the boards of hard, green oak.

One afternoon, my mother got restless. She couldn't lie in bed examining her arrowheads one minute longer. Sneaking downstairs, she bumped into Josie coming inside with a basket of laundry. Normally, Josie was in charge of discipline, but this was such a serious offense that she summoned Cal from the fields. He carried my mother back upstairs, held her in the air by her wrists, and beat her with his belt, determined that his daughter would not end up a cripple. My mother was so upset she stopped speaking to him, even though that meant wetting the bed while she waited for Josie to return from market. At the time, Cal tried not to trouble himself much about the whole episode. He was sure she'd forgive him when she was older, when she could see he'd done it for her own good.

Labor Day came and went, and still Lyle worked on the house. His final project was to paint the exterior, a huge job that involved scraping off the old paint, repairing broken clapboards, sanding the wood, treating it with a mixture of linseed oil and turpentine, and then finally priming and painting. He hired a third man, but even with the extra help, the job took longer than expected. They worked every day, six days a week, starting at dawn. Sometimes they attached floodlights to the scaffolding and worked into the evening. I begged him to slow down, but Cal was pushing him to finish. "What am I supposed to do?" Lyle said. "He wants it done yesterday."

I'd taken the semester off to stay home full-time with Cal. His spells had worsened, and he was growing more anxious by the day. I reminded him that treatment had gotten a lot better since the Colonel's time, that some doctors even believed a cure was near, but it was clear he just wanted to get it over with. After my golf lesson, he often had me drive him to the cemetery, where he stood at the graves of my mother and Josie, telling them, I imagined, that he'd be with them soon.

It was late September when Lyle finally sealed the last bucket of paint and dismantled the scaffolding. That afternoon, my grandfather was to meet with his attorney to finalize his will. As the two of us stood in the yard admiring the house, I told him he should leave the farm to his sister, who lived out West. "The house, the land, whatever," I said.

"I don't want it." He fixed me with a fierce look: There I was, the one person who mattered to him, making things even harder. But I didn't care. He was hurting me, and I wanted him to know it. He told me he and Josie had worked all their lives to make sure my mother would be taken care of once they were gone. "You're her daughter," he said, "so like it or not, it's all coming to you."

When the lawyer arrived, I slipped into Cal's workshop, pocketed the pill bottle from his tackle box, and told him I needed to run some errands. My plan was to see Dr. Miller and tell him what Cal intended to do, but after an hour in the parking lot at the VA, staring at the pill bottle on my dashboard, I lost my nerve imagining the look on Cal's face if he found out I betrayed him to a doctor. I spent the rest of the day driving around with a pint of vodka between my knees, eventually making my way out to Lexington, across the dam to Irmo, and then up Highway 5 toward White Rock. I wanted to see the little lake house where I'd lived with my parents before my mother's accident. I hadn't been there in years, and at first I thought I'd made a wrong turn in the shadowy dusk. But it turned out the house was gone, as were the other cottages that had once dotted the shore, and in their place stood a row of condominiums overlooking the lake. Also gone was our rickety dock. Now five new docks pointed like fingers into the cove, each one ringed by expensive-looking sailboats.

By then, of course, it had begun to rain. For weeks I'd been praying for a storm, rain being the only thing that would have slowed Lyle's crew, but the late summer sky had stayed clear and blue. Lights shone in a couple of the con-dos; figuring the weather would keep people inside, I took a seat at the end of a dock, letting my feet dangle in the water. Across the lake, lightning speared the sky.

My mother's accident happened on the day after the Fourth of July. The night before, she and my father had hosted their annual cookout, a big bash that involved a bonfire, sev-eral coolers of Schlitz, roman candles, and loud music from the eight-track player in my father's Firebird, which he parked near the lake's edge. While the grown-ups drank and danced the shag, I wandered along the moonlit bank until I found myself staring up at a neighbor's tree house. On a sagging platform that jutted out over the water, I sat watching the party, indistinct figures moving in the firelight. It had been maybe ten minutes when my mother noticed I was missing. After she checked the house, she stood at the end of the dock and called my name. There was real fear in her voice, and it sent a shiver through me. I climbed down and ran to her as fast as I could, calling out all the way, I'm coming, I'm coming.

When I was done with the vodka, I tossed the bottle into the lake, along with my grandfather's pills. By then it was late, almost ten, and the drizzle had turned to a downpour. I hardly noticed. On the way into town, I rolled down the windows and hit ninety miles an hour, the highway tighten-ing around me like a tunnel as raindrops pelted the wind-shield. It's a miracle I made it to Lyle's.

"Where've you been?" he said, answering the door in his boxers.

"Nowhere." I wrung water from my shirt. "Out for a drive."

He fetched a towel while I slipped off my sandals and emptied the soggy contents of my pockets onto his kitchen counter. He was not happy about my going AWOL. He'd been calling the farm all day, and when nobody answered, he'd driven out to check on us. He found my grandfather sitting out front with a pitcher of bloody marys, waiting. He had his days mixed up; he thought it was Friday.

"That's my grandfather," I said. "Knows he wants a drink even if he doesn't know the day." I opened the refrigerator and helped myself to a beer as Lyle went on about how embarrassed Cal had been when he realized his mistake.

"I'm just glad he was okay," Lyle said. "I mean, at first I was almost afraid to go out there."

I had to roll my eyes at that. "If you're so afraid of him dying, why don't you get off your ass and do something?"

Lyle got up from the table and went into the bedroom to find some dry clothes. He was not going to fight with a drunk. "It's been a blast," I said, taking another swallow of beer and putting my sandals back on, but my keys were gone. Lyle had them, and he wouldn't give them back. "I don't think driving is a good idea," he said. When it finally sank in that he was serious, I locked him out of the bedroom and told him to sleep on the sofa. Then I lay in his bed, staring at the shadow of his feet beneath the door and waiting for him to come get me. I wanted him to pick the lock, climb the fire escape, kick down the door, stop at nothing. But he just stood there knocking and asking me to open up, and eventually he went away. I heard him rummaging through the closet, getting blankets and a pillow. I couldn't believe he would give up so easily. I was sure he'd be back, but after a few minutes, the light clicked off.

My mother loved water-skiing and swimming in the ocean and horseback riding, but most of all she loved to race stock cars. Before I was born, she was a two-time track champion in the hobby division at Columbia Speedway, the only lady driver among men who hated racing against a woman and hated losing to one even more. Cal told me she'd always liked driving fast, even before she got her license. Back then he owned an old delivery truck he'd modified to haul silage. In the fields along the edge of the swamp, he grew corn for his cows. He'd cut the corn while it was still green and pack it into a bunker silo, then cover it with a sheet of plastic until it fermented, at which point he'd drain the runoff into silage troughs that ran to the cattle lot at the back of the dairy building.

But first the corn had to be hauled up to the silo, a job my mother volunteered for as soon as she was able to reach the truck's clutch. Even driving full-tilt with the windows down, it was sweltering work, the piedmont sun beating down on the cab until the steering wheel burned her fingers. One day when the mercury hit 102, my mother decided she'd had enough: she convinced a farmhand to help her take off the driver's-side door, claiming it was Cal's idea. They left it leaning against the milk house. My grandfather said it was a wonder she didn't kill herself that day, no seatbelt and no door, nothing but her grip on the wheel to keep her from flying into the air. The sight of her barreling like a madwoman up out of the swamp scared him so badly that he never let her drive the truck again. In fact, even after she got her license, he wouldn't let her drive the family Plymouth unless he was with her. My mother only made things worse when she borrowed the Plymouth and took her friends for a joyride that ended in a ditch along Bluff Road. Still, she would not be denied a car. As soon as she graduated from high school, she took a job in the parts department of the local Ford dealership, moved out, and bought herself an old convertible. Within a few years, she talked her boyfriend into getting her a race car, a '62 Fairlane, and began to make a name for herself at the track. Several times she invited Cal to come see her race, but she was still his little girl, and he could not bring himself to go.

The morning after I stole my grandfather's sleeping pills, I found my keys in Lyle's desk and snuck out while he was in the shower. Cal was already up when I got home. He came out of the bathroom holding his ivory-handled straight edge, his face half covered in shaving cream.

"You're bleeding," I said.

He dabbed his throat, smeared red between his fingers, winked at me. "Think a man could slit his own throat?"

I decided to hide the razor first chance I got—that, his shotgun shells, his hunting knife, whatever I could find. In the kitchen, I was getting a glass of tomato juice and some Tylenol when Cal appeared in galoshes, a fleck of tissue stuck to his Adam's apple. He said it was too wet for golf, that we should hunt arrowheads instead, and I agreed, thinking this might be our last time. The rain had finally stopped. Beyond the dairy building, the fog was just starting to lift, and the land smelled as rich as it had in my childhood, in the long-ago days when Cal used to spot arrowheads from high on the tractor as he dressed the fields. He'd taught me the best time to find them was after a storm, when the points gleamed white in the dark soil. We started at the barn and worked our way toward the bluff. Cal was in high spirits. He didn't mention Lyle's embarrassing visit the day before, nor did he comment on what poor shape I was in, wincing against the daylight, clinging to a thermos of coffee. Now that the house was done, he said, he wanted to celebrate by taking Lyle and me out to dinner.

"Ah," I said. "The Last Supper."

"Sure," he said. "We could do the lamb and leavened bread. But actually I was thinking fried shrimp and hush puppies at Captain's Calabash."

"Okay." I kept walking, wishing away the pain behind my eyes. We'd almost reached the bluff when he cleared his throat and asked me if, by the way, I wouldn't mind putting back his pills.

"I can't," I said. "I threw them in the lake."

He considered this as we turned and started back toward the barn. The sun had finally burned through the clouds, and wisps of steam were rising like ghosts from the wet earth. Behind us, at the edge of the swamp, crows cawed among the cypress and loblolly pines.

"You think I'm making a mistake," he said.

I held my breath and tried to focus on the muddy furrow

at my feet. This was the first time he'd asked me point-blank what I thought. "I don't know," I said. "I just know I don't want you to do it."

Cal looked like he'd been expecting as much. He sighed a tired sigh and said he didn't want anybody having to take care of him. He'd been through all that with his father, and he wouldn't wish it on anyone.

"What if I want to take care of you?"

He knelt to pick up what looked to be a small quartz arrowhead, my question too ridiculous to answer, but as he wiped mud from the stone with his thumb, I kept after him, saying that I didn't see the hurry and that he should wait until he was truly sick, and besides, what ever happened to making the most of what you had left? Didn't he want to be with me as long as he could? He gave me a disapproving gaze, a look I imagine my mother saw a lot of.

"The only reason the Colonel didn't shoot his lights out is because he forgot to. That's not going to happen to me."

"Then why don't you let me help?" This was an idea that had been in the back of my mind for years, but until now I'd had the sense to keep it there. With a grunt, Cal hauled himself to his feet and sized me up, trying to decide if I really thought I was serious. At the moment, I suppose I did. "I could give you the pills myself," I said. "When the time comes."

This got him laughing, which turned into coughing, which reminded him of the crumpled pack of Winstons in his shirt pocket. He lit one up and played along. "And when would that be?"

I unscrewed the thermos and sipped lukewarm coffee. This question was, of course, the reason I'd always kept the idea to myself, all the answers I could think of—when he could no longer remember his own name, no longer dress himself, no longer feed himself—being so arbitrary as to seem absurd, because how could I ever really know when his life was no longer worth living?

"You tell me," I said.

He couldn't help smiling at that, too, but it was a sad smile that didn't last—and I could see I was getting to him. After all those years wishing he'd done better by my mother, all those years trying not to make the same mistakes with me, now it came down to this: Would he or would he not abandon me? I understood that I was using his love for me like a crowbar, trying to pry a promise out of him by making one I'd never keep, but I couldn't stop myself. "Don't you care how I feel?"

"Of course I do." There was no longer irony in his voice, only resignation. He exhaled smoke, stared across the fields. "Okay. We'll do it your way."

"Okay?" I said. "You mean it?"

"What'd I just say?" He finished examining the stone and passed it to me with a shrug. It might have been a chipped spear point, or it might have just been a piece of quartz—neither of us could tell, but I put it in my pocket and carried it home.

Captain's Calabash was no five-star affair, but my grandfather was old-fashioned, and going out to dinner with him meant dressing up even if most of the other patrons were in jeans. He wore his favorite seersucker suit, and I wore a blue cocktail dress I'd bought for rush. On the answering-machine message Cal left for Lyle, he advised him to look sharp as well, but Lyle didn't call back. He didn't return my call, either, the breathless message I'd left telling him about Cal's change of heart. That surprised me—I figured he'd race over as soon as he got the news—but I wasn't going to let Lyle's absence spoil our dinner.

My grandfather was another story. "What's keeping Lyle?" he said, checking his watch. "Think he got my call?" We were sitting in a corner booth beneath a mounted swordfish, picking at an appetizer plate of steamed clams. So far, the evening didn't feel like much of a celebration. Cal had shown little interest in anything except his wine. All day, I'd been trying to cheer him up. I wanted to believe I hadn't talked him into anything, that in the end, he was just like anyone else, in no hurry to die; I wanted to believe he was no more able to let go of me than I was of him. "You and Lyle," he said, "you aren't fighting?" I refilled his glass and tried to change the subject, talking about things we might do now that the house was finished. Cal just nodded along as I suggested a week at the beach, a trip to California to see his sister. It wasn't until Lyle rolled into the restaurant at six-thirty, full of apologies, that Cal finally perked up. Lyle explained he'd been out shopping for a suit, then hustled around town looking for a tailor who could do alterations on the spot.

"Didn't find one," he said, wiggling his arms inside the long sleeves of his jacket.

"You look fine," Cal said.

"For a circus clown," I added, but Lyle was in too good a mood to take offense. You could tell a weight had been lifted from his shoulders: The end of his work hadn't meant the end of Cal after all. Once we placed our orders, Cal excused himself to go to the bathroom. Lyle turned to me.

"Well?"

I feigned interest in the swordfish. "I guess he realized he was being selfish. Not that you'd ever have told him so."

"So the stranger who showed up at my apartment last night," Lyle said, "she's still with us?"

"You should wash your sheets," I said. "They still smell like turpentine. And you shouldn't have let me sleep alone."

He picked up a cocktail napkin and waved it like a white flag. "Ten-four. Won't happen again."

I wasn't going to let him off so easily, but he looked like he meant it, and when Cal came out of the bathroom and smiled at the sight of us together, I couldn't stay mad. The night turned into a celebration after all. We ended up with more food than three people could possibly eat—baskets of hush puppies and popcorn shrimp, platters of broiled oysters, scallops, flounder. Cal was in top form, ordering a bottle of champagne and flirting with the waitresses even more than usual. He brought up my idea of spending a week at the beach and declared that all three of us should go. "I've got a friend with a house at Surfside," he said. "We'll rent a boat, do some crabbing." Watching him preside over the table, seeing him in such an expansive mood, I knew I'd done the right thing. We'd still have months together, maybe years.

After dinner, Lyle followed us back to the farm for a

nightcap, at which time Cal suggested a round of golf in the morning. We'd play at Forest Acres, then have lunch in the clubhouse. I told him I wasn't ready to play in front of other people, but he just clinked his brandy glass against mine and told me to follow his lead. "Remember," he said, "you can observe a lot just by watching."

Shortly after I came to live with my grandfather, I decided to join my mother in heaven. My father had been gone for weeks, and though I'd not yet given up on him, I wanted to punish him for leaving me, and I wanted to punish my grandfather for thinking he could take my parents' place. With half a peanut butter sandwich in my shirt pocket, I climbed out the dormer window of my bedroom and onto the roof. Below me, the propane tank glowed dull in the moonlight, a soft patter of raindrops on its metallic surface. My plan was to jump, but after I stood there awhile, gauging the distance between me and the ground, I decided to run away to heaven instead. From the corner of the roof, I was able to reach the chinaberry tree, but as I shimmied past Cal's window, the branches scraped glass. By the time I reached the wet grass he was there, smoking a cigarette and looking at me like I was a mule. He took my hand and led me back inside, where he toweled my hair, helped me into dry pajamas, and tucked me into bed. On his way out, he stopped at the door. "Look here," he said. "If you want to run away, I'm not going to stop you. I'm getting too old for that." Then he shut off the light.

But the next morning, in spite of himself, he was up at the

crack of dawn with his tools. He nailed my screen shut, pruned the chinaberry tree so that its branches no longer reached the roof, and installed deadbolt locks on the doors. For weeks, he slept with the keys on a string around his neck, and unlike my mother, who in my place probably would have stolen them while he slept, I was comforted by the thought that he wanted to keep me close, that I was too precious to be let go.

After we finished our brandy, Lyle and I went back to his apartment and got busy making up for the previous night. We ended up oversleeping and had to hurry to the farm the next morning, when we were supposed to meet Cal. As soon as we turned off Bluff Road, I knew something wasn't right. The newspaper was still in the yard, the porch light still on. Inside, the house was silent, save the ticking of the cuckoo clock on the mantel.

We called an ambulance, but it was too late. Cal sat slumped in his recliner, an empty pill bottle and rock glass on the table beside him. He still had his suit on, and as he sat there, motionless, it seemed as if the wide lapels were pressing down, pinning him against the worn upholstery. He did not look peaceful so much as deflated, his lips parted where the air had left him.

While Lyle was talking to 911, I held Cal's hand like I should have done when he died—like he would have wanted me to, though of course he'd never have asked. I was crying so hard and so loud that Lyle had to take the phone into the bathroom. It was bad enough that Cal was gone, but to think he'd died alone because of me, because I'd left him no choice but to go behind my back, that was almost more than I could take. My tears were making a spotty mess of his trousers. His skin was already cold, his fingers stiff. I would learn later that he'd been dead for hours, that he'd probably taken the pills as soon as we left.

When Lyle got off the phone, he came back into the den and put his arms around me. In between sobs, I tried to make him understand this was all my fault, but he kept insisting I wasn't to blame, that regardless of what I'd said or done, things had turned out more or less the way Cal planned—he'd simply done what he thought was best, and we had to accept that. I knew Lyle was right, but even so, it would be a long time before I could forgive any of us. He was still holding me when the medics arrived, sirens splitting the morning air. "Careful," he said, gently prying my fingers loose from Cal's. "You don't want to bruise him."

About the Author

Will Allison's debut novel, *What You Have Left*, was selected for Barnes & Noble Discover Great New Writers, Borders Original Voices, and Book Sense Picks, and was named one of 2007's notable books by the *San Francisco Chronicle*. His short stories have appeared in magazines such as *Zoetrope: All-Story, Glimmer Train*, and *One Story* and have received special mention in the *Pushcart Prize* and *Best American Short Stories* anthologies. He is the former executive editor of *Story*. Born in Columbia, South Carolina, he now lives with his wife and daughter in New Jersey. Learn more about Will Allison at www.willallison.com.